"We're supposed to be newlyweds."

"We *are* newlyweds. Marriage is hard. First twelve hours are the hardest." Leah continued typing away, not looking at him.

"So it seems. But we must attempt to make this look real."

"It *is* real. As you pointed out, I signed a license. I took vows. It's all real."

"You know what I mean."

"Love," she said, looking up at him. "You want it to look like love. You want me to gaze at you in adoration so no one doubts my happiness or your penis size. I got it."

His throat tightened, a strange kind of heat prickling his face. "You do not normally talk this way."

"Maybe I do, Ajax—how would you know? We don't know each other. I didn't think you were as big of a jerk as you played it this morning, but, hey, I learned something new. And you think I'm a child, but you're wrong about that, too."

All about the author...
Maisey Yates

MAISEY YATES knew she wanted to be a writer even before she knew what it was she wanted to write.

At her first job she was fortunate enough to meet her very own tall, dark and handsome hero, who happened to be her boss, and promptly married him and started a family. It wasn't until she was pregnant with her second child that she found her very first Harlequin Presents® book in a local thrift store—by the time she'd reached the happily ever after, she had fallen in love. She devoured as many as she could get her hands on after that, and she knew that these were the books she wanted to write!

She started submitting, and nearly two years later, while pregnant with her third child, she received The Call from her editor—at the age of twenty-three she had sold her first manuscript to the Harlequin Presents® line, and she was very glad that the good news didn't send her into labor!

She still can't quite believe she's blessed enough to see her name on not just any book, but on her favorite books.

Maisey lives with her supportive, handsome, wonderful, diaper-changing husband and three small children, across the street from her parents and the home she grew up in, in the wilds of southern Oregon. She enjoys the contrast of living in a place where you might wake up to find a bear on your back porch, then walk into your home office to write stories that take place in exotic, urban locales.

Other titles by Maisey Yates available in ebook:

Maisey Yates

HIS RING IS NOT ENOUGH

HARLEQUIN PRESENTS®

Recycling programs
for this product may
not exist in your area.

ISBN-13: 978-0-373-13179-2

HIS RING IS NOT ENOUGH

First North American Publication 2013

Copyright © 2013 by Maisey Yates

Printed in U.S.A.

HIS RING IS NOT ENOUGH

CHAPTER ONE

"IT'S OFFICIALLY TIME to panic." Leah Holt finished reading her sister's text message and looked up at her father.

The expression on his face could only be described as shock, and Leah really couldn't blame him. She felt the same way. Everyone was here. Everything was planned. The decorations were in place, the cake was made. The media had been alerted and was out in full force. The groom was present and ready.

And the bride was gone.

"Why is it time to panic?" her father, Joseph Holt, asked.

She took a slow breath. She found she didn't want to tell her father. Didn't want to expose Rachel to censure. Because as upsetting as the text was, Leah knew Rachel well enough to know she wouldn't have done this without a very compelling reason. "She's gone. She's…she's not coming."

"Who is not coming?"

Leah looked up and her heart stopped. Ajax Kouros had chosen that precise moment to walk into the room, already dressed in a dark tuxedo, perfectly fitted to his masculine physique. He looked as untouchable as ever. A god more than a man.

Seeing him made her think of summer days at the estate. Of following him around and chatting his ear off. Her sister away at school, her father busy with work, her mother having tea with friends.

But Ajax had always been there to listen. Her sounding board. The one person she'd felt had understood her.

A lot of time had passed between then and now. She wasn't that girl anymore. Not foolish enough to think that a man like Ajax could be interested in her, or what she had to say. And he wasn't that boy, tanned from working shirtless in the sun.

He was a billionaire now. One of the world's most successful businessmen.

And today was the day he was marrying her sister. And officially gaining control of Holt Industries, along with a hefty piece of *her* own business, since so many of her shares were owned by her father's corporation.

At least, it was supposed to be the day he was marrying her sister and gaining control of Holt.

But Rachel was gone. Gone and not coming back, if her text was an indication. And it should be, since it said she was gone and not coming back.

It was so out of character for her bright, beautiful sister. The eternal hostess and darling of the media had never once set a toe out of line. She was always gorgeous and graceful, a walking photo-op.

So very unlike Leah, who was a walking photo-op for a whole different reason. And the press loved to play it up. Loved to highlight her every shortfall, her every imperfection.

Leah swallowed hard and met Ajax's eyes. They were dark, hard. They always had been. Even when he'd been a boy, there had been no laughter there. No lightness. But the darkness was compelling to her, just as it had always been.

"Rachel isn't coming," she said, her voice barely a whisper, but deafening in the empty sitting room of her family estate.

"What do you mean she isn't coming?" he asked, his voice soft, a vein of granite running through it.

"It's just… She texted me. She… Here." She handed the phone to Ajax, nearly dropping it when his fingers brushed hers. "It says she wants to be with Alex, whoever that is, and that she can't marry you. Not now. She's sorry."

"I can read, Leah, but thank you." He handed the phone back to her, and she curled her fingers around it, holding it down at her side. He looked to her father. "Did you know?"

Joseph shook his head. "Did I know what? That she was having second thoughts? Not at all. I never pressured her to do this, Ajax. You know I wouldn't have. I was under the impression she was completely on board with this."

Ajax nodded once, then looked at Leah. "Did *you* know?"

"No." If she'd known, she would never have let things go this far. She would never have let Rachel leave Ajax like this, without warning. With the world watching.

"Alex who?" he asked, his tone sharp. "What other information is there?"

"I…" Leah scrolled back through her phone's messages. The look on Ajax's face was fierce, feral, like nothing she'd ever seen before. Usually he was so controlled, so unruffled. But now he was frightening. A different man entirely. "She doesn't say."

"Text her. Now."

"Ajax, if she needs space…" Her father spoke tentatively.

"I'm not overly concerned about that," Ajax bit out.

Leah texted as quickly as she could, her fingers shaking. Alex who? Anyone I know?

You don't know him. Alex Christofides. Unexpected. And I'm sorry.

"Alex Christofides."

Ajax and her father shared a look that said volumes. The hair on the back of her neck prickled, goose bumps rising on her skin as she realized the full implication of the name.

"Alexios," Leah said slowly. "Alexios Christofides."

"That would be the one," Ajax said. "Not content with attempts to destroy my business, the bastard has to destroy my wedding, as well. And make a grab for Holt, I imagine."

"Why, Ajax? Why does he have it in for you like this?"

A shadow passed over Ajax's face. "I don't know. Just business, I suppose."

"But she… Does she know that? Does she know who he is?"

"She wouldn't," Ajax said. "This isn't her world."

No. But it was hers. She knew about Alexios Christofides and his attempts to bump Ajax's retail and manufacturing conglomerate off the map, via covert stock purchases and reporting of illegal activities that hadn't even existed, much less been provable. Alexios had been a headache for Ajax in an increasingly alarming way over the past five years.

"And you never mentioned him to her?"

"As I said," he replied, teeth clenched, "it is not her world."

Leah sent another text to Rachel, while her father and Ajax continued talking.

He's an enemy of Ajax's. Didn't you know that? What if he's using you?

It's too late, L. Can't marry Jax now. I need to be with Alex.

The day of your wedding?

I'm sorry. Trust me. There isn't another way.

"If Rachel has chosen him," her father broke in, "then she's chosen him."

"Even if he's out to hurt Ajax? And what about the company? My business is rolled into this. I am going to get steamrolled by his heavy machinery tactics."

"You're making the assumption that he doesn't care for Rachel. And that Rachel is a fool. I don't believe that, Leah," her father said.

No. Of course not. Rachel would never be so foolish. At

least, that's what everyone would think. Sparkling, poised Rachel, who did so well in every social situation, would never be seduced away from the man she was meant to marry through lies and deceit. She was too savvy.

Leah didn't buy it. Her sister was wonderful. And as such had been coddled by the media. Rachel didn't see the ugly things in life. And the idea that a man, Alexios, might be lying to her, using her, made Leah's stomach churn.

"Sign it over to me," Ajax said, his attention on Joseph. "Revise the agreement."

"I would," Joseph said. "But the company is something that was promised to my daughters. To the husband of the first to be married."

"It was always meant to be me," Ajax said. "You made the offer with me in mind."

"Yes. Naturally, I assumed it would be you. But what can I do? I gave my word, and I would not have Rachel feel I was holding the company hostage to make her marry the man I wanted her to. And if this is her choice, it's her right to have the company in this matter if she chooses. She knows the agreement, too."

Leah knew the agreement, the promise, had only ever been intended for Ajax and Rachel. Joseph loved Ajax like the son he'd never had, and he and Rachel had seemed like a logical and clear match from moment one. As though Ajax was always meant to be a part of their family.

But now everything was falling apart. And Leah's stores, her business, her entire life, were all wrapped up in the package that might now be delivered into the hands of Ajax's enemy.

If Alex was making a grab for Holt, intent on wrapping his hand around it and crushing it for vengeance against Ajax, then he was going to crush Leah's dreams along with it.

She wasn't the media darling. She wasn't the beautiful one. She wasn't the one who attracted men. She had Leah's Lollies. Her business was on the upswing, building and becoming a sort of trend. Candy from one of her stores was fast becoming one of the most popular gift items in the world. Tiffany Blue might be iconic, but Leah Pink was starting to gain momentum.

She wouldn't lose it. She couldn't. It was who she was.

"I need to talk to Ajax alone," she said, before she could fully process her request. "Please," she said to her father.

He nodded once. "If you must." He looked at Ajax. "I am sorry, my son. But I cannot force her down the aisle. No matter that I wouldn't have had her leave you today, I won't force her. And if she has chosen Alex, no matter who he is to you, if she is intent on him, I won't stop that, either."

"I would never ask that of you," Ajax said, his voice hard.

Her father turned and walked out of the room, and Leah fought the urge to follow him. To try to reason with him. It would be easier than dealing with Ajax. But her father wouldn't bend on this. He had given his word, and in Joseph Holt's world, one where men had honor, one where men didn't stoop so low as to use a woman as part of a business firefight, your word was all that was needed.

But that wasn't the real world. She knew it. Ajax knew it.

Ajax pushed his hand through his hair and looked out the window again. "The question is, what is to be done? There is an agreement, drawn up and ready to sign. There is a wedding planned. There are a thousand guests coming in only three hours. The media will be there. This has been hailed as the wedding of the century. So the question is—" he turned to face Leah "—what is to be done?" His control was fraying slightly, an edge to his voice that Leah wasn't accustomed to.

She looked at his face, at the hard lines around his mouth. At the worry in his eyes. Ajax Kouros, worried. And the answer hit her. So clear, so simple. This was how things worked in business, and what they were dealing with was a business-related problem. A contract that needed signing.

Or to be specific, two contracts that needed signing.

"What was the extent of your deal? What did the contract say?"

"Ownership of Holt was to pass to me upon signing the wedding agreement, contingent on the fact that the marriage last for five years. Otherwise, ownership returns to your father."

"And the names on the document?"

"No names. Interchangeable. That's the issue."

"Five-year minimum?"

"Yes."

"I'll do it," Leah said.

The words hung in the room, too loud in the emptiness.

For one fleeting moment she felt exposed. Awkward. No. She wasn't that girl anymore. She was stronger than that. She'd learned. Never expose yourself. Never let them see you cry.

"You will do what?" Ajax asked, dark eyes now trained on her.

"I…" Insecurity rose up and grabbed her by the throat, choking her. Past Leah, the Leah who had idolized Ajax. The girl had made a fool of herself chasing after his attention, his affection. The idiotic teenager who had nearly declared herself just before he'd declared his love for Rachel.

It's for Leah's Lollies. It has nothing to do with those feelings. It's for Holt.

She wasn't a slave to those old feelings anymore. Sure, she'd dreamed of Ajax when she was a girl, but then, like everyone else, he'd chosen Rachel. And she'd learned never to expose herself like that again. Had learned how to cover up pain under a layer of armor. Because the alternative was to show it to the world, and damn your pride.

Well, she was quite fond of her pride.

"I'll marry you. And then the guests and the companies, yours, mine and Holt, and all of that will be fine. And no matter what, no matter if Rachel marries Christofides next month or…tomorrow, it won't be him that gets his hands on Holt. It will be okay. All of it."

He laughed, humorless, dark. "It will all be fine, will it? Perfection. Just a slight hiccup."

"I'm well aware this is more than a hiccup. But it's better than nothing, right?"

Ajax was not an expressive man. He'd been good to her sister, but not overly affectionate. She'd wondered more than once exactly what sort of relationship they had. If it was more convenience than passion. But just then, she had to acknowledge that Ajax looked very much like a man who'd lost the love of his life.

Ajax put his fingers through his hair again, the look in his eyes so different to what she was used to. Lost. It reminded her of a younger version of him. Of the boy he'd been before coming to the Holt Estate. A boy she'd never known.

She still remembered the moment she'd met him, when they'd come to the estate for the summer. It was like the world had fallen away. Like *she'd* fallen away.

She'd been so young, but there had been something about him that had pulled her to him. He'd, in an instant, been so many things to her. And he'd listened. He'd made her feel important. Special. And she'd clung to him, followed him around like a lost puppy. Obvious. Just thinking about it made her skin crawl with embarrassment.

He looked at her, that lost look in his eyes fading as suddenly as it had appeared. Now his gaze was unreadable, unexpressive. Like he was looking over a new yacht, or sports car. Well, no, not even that. He got a bit more passionate over sports cars. And dark chocolate. That was one thing they had in common. Or at least something they'd had in common.

Handy, because she was short on sports cars, but she did have a lot of dark chocolate. Occupational hazard. Although, she'd stopped trying to tempt him with treats a while ago. About the time she'd realized she was staring at him like an idiot and _he_ only had eyes for her sister.

"You will have to do."

The way he said it made her want to melt into a puddle and slither out of the room. She was being compared to Rachel, again, and being found utterly lacking. "Thanks. And you're welcome."

"Don't expect me to be happy about any of this." He started to pace. "My bride has walked out on me. Chosen my rival over me. And she didn't even have the courtesy to text *me* about it. Rather she contacted you."

"I'm her sister."

"And I'm the man she was supposed to love," he bit out.

She put her hand on his arm, a flash of heat racing from her fingertips and through her body. She pulled back as though she'd been burned.

She hadn't expected that. Hadn't expected to feel that intense, scorching heat. After all, she'd stopped carrying a torch for Ajax years ago. Though, that didn't change the fact that he was an incredibly handsome man. The heat was only due to a physical attraction. She was only human. She imagined any woman who touched him would feel the same way.

Thank God she knew how to hide that moment of insanity. She'd spent years cultivating her mask, one that kept the press at a distance. One that kept her from getting hurt. One of indifference. A smooth, cutting smile on hand whenever she needed it. One that said: *Oh, you again. Can't be bothered.*

Oh, dear Lord. I proposed to him.

That thought made her smile slip.

But it wasn't as if she'd done it for herself. Not for herself personally, anyway. Everything was on the line. The future of Holt, of Leah's Lollies, and Ajax's dreams and hard work. And that mattered to her. She wasn't in love with him anymore, hadn't been for years. But she cared. About Holt. About her own business.

"Why, Leah? What are you getting out of this?"

"Well, jeez, Ajax, Rachel has clearly lost her mind. She's run off with this man that you and I both know is probably not with her by coincidence. A man who would do this just to hurt you. He would, wouldn't he?"

"Yes," he said.

"My father loves Rachel, but he's frankly blind to her faults."

"Does she have them?" Ajax asked dryly.

"She's far too trusting, I think, which you and I know full well is a fault. Alexios would take advantage of that to get to you and to get his hands on Holt to keep you from expanding your business. He'll hurt her. And I can't allow that. I doubt you can, either."

"Of course not."

"So then it's settled. We have to marry before she does. You can still graft yourself into my family tree, which we both know you want. Otherwise we both lose Holt. You especially lose. You lose Rachel, *and* Holt, to Christofides."

"I didn't know Holt mattered to you so much, Leah."

"In terms of it being my family legacy, it does. I can't just let it pass into some stranger's control. But more than legacy, my father owns half the stock in my business, and it's all rolled into the Holt corporate umbrella. Suddenly a stranger has control over me and my business."

"And if Rachel wants Holt?"

"She doesn't. It doesn't mean to her what it means to you and me—you know that. She was going to be your right hand socially, but I doubt she ever spent a day in those offices of her own free will."

"True enough. But I didn't require that of her. A hostess, someone to give me a softer face—*that* I needed."

She looked at the granite lines etched by his mouth, his eyes. Yes, he most certainly did need a hostess.

She took a breath, putting her hard, practiced expression in place. "Well, that's not happening now. And do you want some other man to have your wife and your business?"

Ajax took a step toward her, dark eyes trained on hers, and she felt something inside her melt.

"Other than Holt, Leah, what do you want?"

"To preserve Leah's Lollies. Holt owns a quarter of my stock. And in addition to my candy stores being linked to Holt, I *am* a Holt. It's my legacy. It's ours, not just yours."

"It was meant to be mine and Rachel's."

"I know."

"And you trust me with your stocks, do you? Alexios is quite the financial genius—perhaps he would serve you better than I would. Rachel seems to think so."

"You'll do right by me and my shops, Ajax. I have no doubt."

"I don't know. Perhaps I'll sell my stocks off. You think they'll be profitable enough for me?"

"Of course I do. I sell things that are expensive and bad for you. I think I'll be in business forever."

He arched a dark brow, something in his expression changing. "A sure success, then. There is very little some people love more than indulging a vice."

"Yes. Well, and if I may, allow me to continue my argument for marriage."

"Please," he said, no emotions on display.

"You're right. Everything is in place. Everything. You taking the reins at Holt. The guests. The minister. The cake. There's… I donated a lot of candy. A gift."

"Nice of you."

"Well, now I'm donating a bride. Which might be a bit more than nice."

"If I accept."

"Oh."

Ajax looked at Leah, the woman who, up until ten minutes ago, had been about to become his sister-in-law. Now she was talking about being his wife. Leah. He scarcely thought of her as a woman. In his mind, she was still a round sixteen-year-old girl with curly hair, braces and a sweet tooth.

He could remember, very clearly, having a piece of candy waiting for him with his gardening tools every day when he'd first started working at the Holt Estate. And what had started as a childish game had continued as a tradition. When he'd started interning at the corporate headquarters in New York there had been a piece of candy on his desk. And when he'd branched off on his own, an entire bouquet, and yes, it could only be described as a bouquet, of chocolate had been waiting in his office.

Yes, whenever one of her little gifts showed up, he pictured Leah, the girl. Sweet, uncomplicated Leah, who looked at him and saw someone worth smiling at. But that vision didn't match the reality standing in front of him.

Now she was a woman, he supposed. She was twenty-three. Some of her roundness had melted away, but not all. Her hair was still a mass of dark curls, albeit sleeker than when she'd been a teenager. And there was a hardness to her that had never been there before.

Still, she was nothing like Rachel. Beautiful, willowy Rachel.

Rachel, the woman he'd set his sights on so many years ago. The woman he'd spent so many years planning to marry. She had been standing there, at the end of his path, his goal, for so long that having her removed left him feeling lost. Aimless.

She was the only woman he'd ever loved.

And she had left him. Along with her, she would take Holt, and every piece of the plan, of his life would be broken off in chunks and scattered around his feet.

If he let it happen. If he didn't accept Leah's offer.

It was a bad day for his pride. That he needed help saving a deal he'd spent years working toward because his bride had decided to skip the wedding, burned. She'd left him to be with someone else. His biggest business rival.

This wedding, their union, made it feel like pieces were finally fitting together. Like the pieces of his life had united into one smooth picture, the end of the plan in sight.

Everything he wanted. Everything he'd worked for, in his

grasp at last. His reward for rigid control, for never deviating from the path since he'd first put his foot down on it.

But Rachel hadn't seen things that way. Obviously.

He supposed, if he thought about it, it made sense. Rachel was passionate. About life, about everything. But she'd never been passionate with him. And she'd never been bothered by his reserve with her. He'd imagined she was responding to the way he was naturally. Now he wondered.

Still, pride wouldn't see his plans come to fruition. They wouldn't bring Rachel back, either. Refusing Leah was of no benefit to him. It simply wasn't logical.

However, he had a hard time thinking of her as a wife. As the sort of woman he would share his life with, take to events, take to bed.

Leah was not the woman he'd imagined himself with. Not ever.

"Well, come on, Ajax, don't keep a girl waiting like this," she said, a small smile curving up the edge of her lips. As though she were unruffled. As though all of this was just an interesting diversion. He wondered when she'd become so calculating. When she'd traded in that sweetness for the hard, cutting edge of a businesswoman.

"I accept." There was no logical reason not to. And above anything else, he was a man of logic. Emotion could never be allowed to rule. "I will make a call and have the seamstress come and fit Rachel's dress to you."

Leah's cheeks turned pink, although her expression remained stone cold. "Could you cut a foot off the hem and add the fabric around the middle?"

She was exaggerating and yet, she had a point. Rachel was long and angular, while the top of Leah's head came just below his shoulder. It could not be ignored; she was certainly a larger size than her sister. Though she wasn't proportioned unattractively. Round in the appropriate places. He'd just never given it much thought.

"What size, then? I will order you a new one."

"I'll make a call," she said, her cheeks still pink. "It will have to be off-the-rack, of course. We only have two hours, but it's doable. All things considered, the fit of my dress will be the least scandalous thing about this wedding."

"You are still a Holt heiress," he said.

"Yes, we're practically interchangeable. Except, clearly, for the dress size."

"That is not what I meant. You are not interchangeable." He gritted his teeth. "You are not Rachel." Rachel, who, in his mind, was the embodiment of his perfect life. He'd imagined that when he reached this day, when he reached her, standing at the head of the aisle, his struggle, his fight to stay on the path, to stay in control, would be over. That he would finally have reached a destination instead of walking endlessly.

He'd never touched her, not beyond a casual kiss, but things between them had been understood, for the past six years. They hadn't spent all of their time together, hadn't acted as a couple. Rachel hadn't wanted to feel tied down. She'd wanted to live her life. But he'd been confident that in the end she would come back to him.

He had been wrong. And he hated being wrong.

"I'm sorry about that. Not that I'm not her, but that she left. I am."

"Of course you are. Now you're stuck with me."

She looked up at him, whiskey-colored eyes glittering. He didn't know why she looked like she was about to cry. Because of the situation? Though she had been part of creating it, it wasn't like he had asked for her to stand in. Or because of his comments? Either way, he didn't like it.

Joseph Holt had become a mentor to him when he'd been a teenager, and his family had, in many ways, become his family. He would never do anything to hurt the Holt family. Ever.

"It is not too late to back out, Leah. I will not hold you to a rash statement made in the heat of an emotional moment."

"It *is* all very emotional."

"I meant for you."

She blinked. "For you, as well. Do you feel nothing?"

"I feel—of course I do. But I do not make decisions based on emotion, which is why I'm prepared to marry you instead of Rachel. It's logical." It kept his plan going until he could shift things. Until he could get everything re-sorted in his mind. Planning kept him on point, in control, and control was everything.

He knew what happened when control was lost. Knew what happened when a man lived for feeling.

"Yes. Well, while the situation overall might be emotional, I didn't offer out of a sense of emotion."

"Holt is mine. By right. By promise. I'm not family by blood, but your father trained me for this."

"I know. And I've worked too hard to elevate Leah's Lollies to this position to see it mowed down in a firefight."

He looked at Leah and wondered if he'd underestimated her. He knew she had a business mind, whereas Rachel most certainly put the *social* in socialite and had used the money her father had given her to become a silent partner in a few ventures that helped expand her web of personal connections.

It was one of the reasons Rachel had been such a valuable prospect for a wife. She did what he did not. She connected with people, made friends easily, and used charisma to make happen what she wanted to see done.

She was, in essence, the perfect accessory to his life. Leah on the other hand, was more focused on the business end. She would possibly want a hand in the decision making at Holt, which would be her right, since ownership was to be shared between him and his wife.

But then, he would get a stake in Leah's Lollies, which, in spite of his line of questioning, he knew was quite successful. And with his assets? Mass production of her products was entirely possible.

In terms of how he would benefit, there was the chance it could be very profitable for him. As for Leah…it could be extremely profitable for her.

"What else do you know, Leah?" he asked.

"A lot. I see things. I know how much this means to you. I know you didn't spend years working under my father to not end up as head of Holt."

It was true. Joseph Holt had become his mentor when he'd been a sixteen-year-old boy with little schooling and no money, working on the grounds of the opulent Holt Estate in Rhodes. He'd only just left his father's mansion, fled the island he'd grown up on, which was filled with so much corruption not even the police could help him. He'd been rooming with other teenagers who'd been disowned by their families, for varying reasons. Working. Paying rent. And he'd protected them all, because he'd known about the evil that was out there waiting.

They'd lived and worked like that until better jobs had taken them better places.

For Ajax, that better place had been provided by Joseph Holt. Every summer and winter, the Holts came and stayed on the estate. Unlike other wealthy families he'd worked for, they'd been kind, friendly with their staff. Especially Joseph Holt, who had taken the time to speak with everyone, get to know everyone.

And he'd taken a special interest in Ajax. Had, in many ways, become the father he'd never had. But more than that, he'd taught him an interest in business. Had sent him to college. Had, like he'd done for his daughters, given him money as venture capital. Ajax had spent three years working at Holt in the United States, and after that, he'd gone on to get his own business off the ground, dealing in retail stores, rather than manufacturing.

Ajax had made his success thanks to Joseph, knowing all the while that in the end, Holt would be a part of his stable of assets. As would Rachel.

He had lost one of those things today; he would not lose the other.

"You do see a lot, Leah. And I think you have inherited your father's ability to spot a good business deal. And his inability to pass it up."

She lifted her chin, dark hair shimmering in the light, the glossy curls sliding from her shoulders to tumble down her back. "I am a Holt, Ajax."

"As is Rachel."

"I am not my sister. Not even close. That you will have to remember."

He looked her over. Still, he couldn't help but see that image of a young teenager, sitting in her father's office with a book on her lap, her hair, not glossy or gently curled, but frizzy and barely contained by a rubber band. Or her following him around the estate, chatting his ear off about a new idea she had for a business, asking him if he thought it might work.

If you put your mind to it, Leah, it will work.

That was what he'd always told her. He hadn't realized how true it was. Just how dangerous she could be when she set her mind on something.

"I am in no danger of forgetting."

"I'll need…" She cleared her throat. "Well, that is, I have to get ready now."

CHAPTER TWO

LEAH'S HANDS SHOOK as she picked up the bouquet, the one that was meant to have been her sister's. Thank God she never could have in a million years worn her sister's dress or shoes.

And this was the first time ever she'd been glad she couldn't have. She didn't want her sister's flowers, groom, dress *and* shoes.

As it was, the dress and shoes were Leah's. The flowers and groom...they weren't.

Her stomach cramped painfully and she looked in the mirror. Her eyes looked overly large for her face, and as frightened as she felt. She didn't have her mask up. Because she was very suddenly confronted with the reality of what she was doing.

On paper, in the moment, it had been very black-and-white. Alexios couldn't be allowed to succeed in gaining access to Holt. If he was using Rachel, it couldn't be a reward.

But here, standing in a wedding dress? It was feeling more real. More insane.

She reached down and took a tissue off the vanity and pressed her lips to it, leaving a crimson stain behind. She stared at it for a moment. Would her lips leave red marks on Ajax's?

And it hit her with the force of a wrecking ball. She was going to kiss him. Today. She sank down onto the chair that was positioned in front of the mirror. She was actually *marrying* him. A legal marriage.

Worse, and more worrisome, since it was in her immediate

future, she was about to expose herself to the press, and their ridicule, again. Her least favorite thing ever.

This wedding was huge. A major event. Rachel was so popular, a style icon for the masses and a favorite on the cover of magazines worldwide. And Ajax…he exuded dark sex appeal and mystery, plus there was the whole billionaire thing. That made this wedding, their wedding, a very big deal.

And she just didn't match up to the fanfare.

She stood up and tried not to topple over as she looked in the mirror. She put her hands over her breasts, barely contained by the bodice of the strapless gown. Not her first choice, but it had been an emergency, and that meant she'd had to take the smaller size, and she'd had to take the one that showed a bit too much of her curves. Which were abundant. And she wasn't big on putting them on display.

So, yay, of course now she'd be doing it in front of an audience of a thousand. Plus photographers. As a replacement bride for the lovely Rachel, who the media showed such favor. Who men, all through their lives, had shown such favor.

It reminded her of the time she'd gone to an event in a dress Rachel had worn earlier in the year. So there Leah was, having the sort of fashion misstep sixteen-year-olds often did, but in front of the world. Her less-svelte figure was too much on display thanks to the dress being too small, and the color washed her out. It had been put in a fashion magazine under a Who Wore it Better? heading. And Leah had been savaged in both the article and online.

Borrowing clothes from her sister's closet was a lot more fraught for her than it was for other teenagers.

She remembered so clearly sitting down and crying in her father's office when she'd seen it, and Ajax coming in. He'd been visiting, taking time out from his own corporate empire that was making a serious statement in the business landscape. But he'd always made time for them. He'd always felt like a part of the Holt family.

"I'm so humiliated, Ajax!" she'd wailed. "How will I ever live this down?"

Ajax had looked at her, dark eyes impassive. "If you don't want to be compared to your sister, stop putting yourself in the position. You're different. You will never be her, so stop trying." He'd knelt in front of her then. "And you must never let them see you cry. Never give them anything they can use against you. An unbreakable target is not a satisfying one."

He was right, then and now. She wasn't Rachel. Not even close. And so she'd made an effort to look as different as possible from her sister. And she'd never let them see her cry.

Leah had become the snarky one, the one with the acerbic wit, the businesswoman who didn't care what the press said and didn't waste time trying to court them.

She'd become her own person. Her own very guarded person.

Unless she was with Ajax. With him, she'd felt free to show herself. She'd poured her heart out to him. Hours spent tailing him at the estate replaced with spending time in his office after school.

And she'd left him treats. Ajax wasn't demonstrative, but she always saw the candy wrappers in the trash bin the next morning. And it always earned her a smile. A small one, but from Ajax, it had been gold.

And with those small smiles a girlish crush had turned into love. She'd been so close to telling him, too. One night when there were few people left in the Holt building and they'd been alone in his office. But she'd lost her nerve.

And by the end of the week, he'd announced that he intended to marry Rachel.

Never let them see you cry.

His words had played over and over in her mind that day, as her dreams, her fantasies, had been crushed like a rose in an iron fist. She hadn't gone to his office after that. She hadn't left any candy on his desk again.

She hadn't shown a crack in her facade since.

But no matter how she played it, she still didn't like what the press wrote about her, and she knew this would be no exception.

Round-ish Candy Tycoon to Wed Man Way Out of Her League in Desperate Last-Minute Substitution at Wedding!

There was a headline she could live without.

But it was likely unavoidable. All right, it wouldn't say round-ish, but still. There would be an implication. Especially since she owned candy stores. They loved that about her. That she'd grown up to sell candy. It made for such delightful headlines, filled with the suggestion that she overindulged in her own product.

And she would be standing there, next to Ajax, who was physical perfection. She was sure she would look like a little marshmallow in comparison. A little marshmallow with cleavage.

"Leah." Her father walked into the room, and Leah whirled around toward the sound of his voice. He looked as shell-shocked as she felt. "Are you ready?"

"Yes."

"Are you sure?"

Leah nodded slowly. "Yes."

She felt dizzy, light-headed.

You know what this is. You signed the agreement. There will be an end date on this marriage. He'll probably never even touch you.

But fantasy and reality were having a head-on collision and it was hard to remember how she was supposed to feel. Who she was supposed to be. It was hard to keep her mask in place while the world shook beneath her feet.

"I want to do this," she said, her voice hushed.

The expression on her father's face changed, as if he was seeing deep inside her. "I see." He extended his arm. "Then let's go. I confess, I was not ready for you to be married yet."

She wanted to shout that he didn't see. Because there was nothing to see. Instead, she cleared her throat. "I'm twenty-three."

"But still. With Rachel I knew it was coming. I was much more ready for her to marry. And I knew…I knew Ajax's intentions for a long time. The moment his feelings toward Rachel changed, he told me."

"Six years," Leah said, knowing the exact moment, the exact hour. Because the memory was still so raw, no matter that it shouldn't be.

"She wanted to live more first. She was only twenty-two when he fell in love with her. And you don't want to live?"

"I can still live with a husband," she said. "I'll be married, not dead." And probably not married for that long. Or in truth.

"That's true. But you are still my baby."

She breathed in deep, fighting against the tight ache in her throat. "Dad, I haven't lived at home in years."

"I know."

"And Ajax is like a son to you."

Her father stopped walking and looked at her. "And if he hurts you, I will personally see him undone."

She blinked. "He won't." She would make sure he wouldn't. Her armor was solid; it wouldn't break now. In spite of her moment of flailing insecurity back in the dressing room, she would make sure her armor held.

Anyway, Ajax didn't have a foothold in her life anymore. Not in her emotions at least. She might still find him physically attractive, but she wasn't hopeless over him anymore.

They stopped talking then, because they were in the foyer, and just beyond that was the courtyard, where everything had been prepared for the wedding. Rachel's wedding. None of it was to her taste. Leah was more whimsical, her sister a sophisticate. Everything was white at Rachel's wedding.

Too damn bad she hadn't shown up.

Leah swallowed hard as the doors opened and the sunlight

poured in, painting her in white, too. The only color was the sea beyond the stone-covered courtyard, a blue jewel against the sun-washed sky.

She started descending the steps, and the guests stood, a gasp and ripple of whispers rustling through the crowd, audible even over the string quartet that was playing. She knew what they were saying. They were wondering why. Why her?

Why not the beautiful sister? Surely, everyone would know Rachel had left. Because there was no way Ajax would have preferred her. And everyone would know that.

She'd always imagined she would marry here. In Rhodes. But it hadn't looked like this in her mind.

She raised her eyes and saw Ajax, standing at the head of the aisle, and her heart just about burst through her chest, nerves, remnants of old dreams converging on her, making it hard to breathe. Ajax had always been in her fantasies. Always. Of course, in her fantasies of old as she drew nearer to him on her trip down the aisle, he had smiled. He hadn't looked at her like she was judge, jury and executioner come to hand him a terrible sentence.

But that's how he looked now. Grim. Like a man at the gallows, not the altar.

She tightened her hold on her father's arm and continued down the aisle, looking anywhere but at Ajax. What was she doing? She couldn't back out. She was halfway down the aisle, the man had already been jilted once today. And as they drew closer, the ache in her heart intensified, a swollen mass of emotion growing in her, choking her.

And logic couldn't talk her out of it. Her mind telling her that she shouldn't feel anything for him, did nothing to stop it.

Where was her armor? How had this sneaked beneath it?

They stopped at the head of the aisle, and Leah just about stopped breathing.

"Who gives this woman to this man?" The pastor's voice was thin, distant. Like he was underwater.

"I do."

Her father sounded the same way, so maybe it was just her.

And then he kissed her cheek and she was moving toward Ajax. He extended his hand, and she took it. He had never held her hand before. Now that she thought about it, she didn't think he'd ever touched her skin.

Heat assaulted her, starting at her cheeks, spreading to her ears. Oh, good. Now she was blushing. What was wrong with her? Why couldn't she get a grip?

Why did this feel so real?

It's not real. It's just business. It's for Leah's Lollies. It's for Holt. It's not for you.

He took her other hand, too, turned her to face him. Terror streaked through her, and on its heels, an emotion so big, so real, she couldn't deny it. Couldn't push it down. It grew, it bloomed in her, alive, strong.

In that moment, reality melted away, and fantasy won out.

Surely this was only a fantasy. With her in a wedding gown and Ajax, looking like perfection in a tux, how could it be anything else? It couldn't be real. This was a dream, the dream she used to have when she was a teenager. It wasn't real.

He said his vows, his voice steady. Strong, without emotion, but then, that was how he was. She spoke hers without stumbling, and there was this strange, underlying conviction that each word was the truth. That there would be no one but him, forever.

There never had been, not for her. It was Ajax. Always.

She could feel the walls inside of her start to quake. Start to crumble. All of that supposed hard edge she'd cultivated. All of her defense.

"You may now kiss the bride."

Leah's heart stopped, and for a moment, so did the world. Her focus dropped to Ajax's lips. How many times had she thought about kissing those lips?

It was her last thought before he wrapped his arm around her waist and dipped his head, his mouth covering hers.

She hadn't been prepared. Not for the heat, the flash of pure fire that raced along her veins. She found herself lifting her arms, curling her fingers around the lapels of his suit jacket.

She'd expected something chaste, something appropriate for a thousand pairs of eyes, for two people who had barely ever touched, but that wasn't what she got. What she got was a real, full-on kiss.

He slid his tongue along the seam of her lips, and she opened eagerly, tasting him as he tasted her. She felt as if she was falling, but Ajax was there to hold her up, his arm a strong band around her waist, her fingers curled into his jacket like claws.

She'd never been kissed like this. Not ever. And she'd never felt like this, either. Like she would die if he stopped touching her, like her skin was on fire. Her breasts ached, her heart fluttering like a trapped bird. And the ache, low and strong between her thighs. An ache she knew only he could satisfy.

And all of her expectations about the marriage were blown apart. And all she had were questions. Well, questions, a thundering heartbeat and the feeling of being horribly, hideously exposed.

And then, suddenly, he pulled away and she nearly lost her balance. The guests were clapping, and the pastor was making his pronouncement, but she couldn't pay attention. Her head was swimming, her legs shaking.

"Smile," Ajax whispered in her ear, and it kick-started her brain again.

Never let them see you cry.

So she did smile, a bright, false smile she didn't feel, and he led her down the aisle as the band played.

They went back up the stairs. Into the house.

The doors closed behind them, and Ajax started loosening his tie.

"Don't we need… Should we… The photographer."

"Do you honestly think I want pictures?" he asked, his voice rough.

"I…I had thought… It's our… We paid for the photographer."

"I'm sure the press in attendance got enough. I am not interested in posing for photos. What I would like is alcohol."

"You don't drink."

"Not usually."

Never. She'd never seen him drink. That wasn't the best for her ego. That marrying her was driving him to drink.

"What about the reception?"

"I am far too eager to take you back to my villa and consummate the marriage," he said, his tone dry as sand. "We'll have to skip it."

"Wh…what?"

"We're leaving. Now." She didn't want to leave now. Not while she felt so…shaken.

But they were.

He took her hand again, and they went out the other direction, out the front doors, where there was a limo idling. He opened the back door for her and she got in. He gathered up the skirt of her dress and put it in behind her before getting in and closing the door.

He looked out the window and she followed his gaze to the photographer standing on the step. "Let's give him a picture," he said, his voice nearly a growl.

"The windows are tinted."

"He'll work around that. It's his job to get the shot after all."

He hauled her to his body, her breasts, precariously close to making an exit from the bodice of her dress, pressed against his hard chest. And then, for the second time in the space of five minutes, she was being kissed by Ajax Kouros.

After consigning Ajax to the "fantasies that were never going to happen" bin, two kisses in such short succession were shocking.

His tongue delved deep, tasting her, sending a shock wave through her, straight to her core. And again, she found herself responding, helplessly, intensely. She speared her fingers through his hair, held on to him for all she was worth.

She couldn't pretend she didn't feel this. Couldn't pretend that the touch of his lips against hers didn't light a fire in her body. Couldn't pretend that no matter what her emotions were doing, no matter how she'd shut them down, she'd never wanted a man the way she wanted Ajax.

He removed his lips from hers and pressed a kiss to her neck, down lower, lower…oh…yes.

Then he lifted his head. "Drive," he said, the order clearly meant for his driver and not for her. He kissed her neck again, his tongue tracing a circle over her skin before the limo exited the driveway of her family's estate and went out onto the main winding road that led back down to the highway.

Then, he moved away from her, all of the heat from the earlier moment completely gone. As if cold water had been thrown on a flame.

"What was…all that?"

"I was not in the mood to deal with questioning—were you?"

"I… No, I suppose not."

"We'll need to get a story together, one that matches, before we talk to the press."

"Right, okay, I see the merit in that." Her lips felt swollen and hot, and she felt dizzy. What had just happened to her? She looked down at her hand, where he'd placed a ring only moments before, and she wondered if she was involved in some kind of weird dream.

"There will have to be an explanation for why it was you and not Rachel who walked down the aisle today."

"And the truth won't work? That she realized she loved someone else?"

The expression in his eyes could only be described as fierce. "No, it does not. Would it be so simple for you?"

"I suppose not. But please let's come up with an answer that doesn't completely burn my pride. I've had enough of that in the media."

"We both have issues of pride, it seems. I do not intend to hurt you, Leah, but none of this was part of my plan."

"Clearly."

"I imagine it wasn't a part of yours, either."

"Well, this morning I was getting ready for my sister's wedding, and it turned out to be *my* wedding. And now I'm married and sitting in a limo on my way to…I don't even know where. Maybe you told me, but I forgot because that's just the kind of day it's been."

"My home. We weren't planning on going on a honeymoon until things had started settling at Holt."

"Are you going to New York?"

He shook his head. "Not yet. But I will be working from my office here on getting things in order. Your father has left everything in magnificent working order, and the transition has been well under way for a while, but even so…"

"Business first. I don't have anything to wear," she said. "I have this dress. I don't have…panties." The words sort of slipped out, horrifying her as they did. She didn't feel savvy, or self-contained, or well-protected. She felt dazed. "I don't have deodorant. My suitcase is back at the house."

"I will have all new clothes sent over if you like. And your things from New York."

"My things from… What?"

"You'll be living here with me. We will of course travel to New York, but we'll stay in my penthouse there, not in your apartment or flat or whatever it is you have."

"It's a very nice apartment."

"We will live together. We are husband and wife after all."

"Oh. Right. Yes. We are."

"You sound shocked."

"Are you not?"

He looked her over, dark eyes assessing. "I am a hard man to shock, Leah, but all things considered, I am a bit."

He was so dry, so condescending. It wasn't fair that he was so in control. That his mask never slipped. Because she was confused and a little freaked and kind of in internal upheaval and he just…wasn't.

He was all cold and calm and stare-y.

Blessed reality was starting to trickle in. Cold. Unflinching. It provided a harsh portrait of her slipups over the past few minutes. Over how stupid she'd let a couple of kisses make her when she knew better than to let that happen. Or, she at least knew better than to let anyone see it. She knew better than to reveal anything.

"You really want me to live with you?" She crossed her arms beneath her breasts, then thought better of it when she realized just how effectively that hoisted them up.

"*Need* is the better word," he said. "I will not risk this appearing to be anything but real." He put his elbow on the armrest of the car and put his hand on his forehead. The first sign of him truly not being all that okay.

They were silent for the rest of the ride to the house. And while they climbed the mountain, anger built inside her. Blessed anger that helped her armor feel fortified.

The limo wound its way up the mountain that would carry them to Ajax's home. She realized she hadn't been there. He came over to the family's estate for parties in Rhodes, and he visited her family's penthouse in New York, but she'd never visited him here, not after he'd got a home.

She'd never seen where he'd lived as a teenager working on the estate, either, but she'd been a child then so it wasn't all that surprising.

Double gates came into view, then they parted as the limo approached. And beyond them was a sleek, modern home with windows that opened it all up to views that surrounded it. Mountains behind, the ocean, glimmering bright in front. Bright pink flowers climbed the walls, the only nod to a traditional Greek villa.

The rest was all new. Clean lines and exceptionally expensive construction.

"I've never been here before," she said.

"Have you not?" A strange look passed over his face.

"No. I haven't. You've never invited me. Well, it's not like we really hang out." *Anymore.* "We just happen to make a wide circle around each other at many of the same gatherings, and kind of, pass close enough two or three times in an evening to say 'lovely to see you, how about this shrimp cocktail? Delightful? Yes, delightful!' But no, we don't hang out."

Not by accident. After her big Ajax-induced heartbreak she'd needed to push him away. Needed to give herself some time to erect stronger barriers.

"And I don't have parties," he said, his voice comically serious.

"So, that mystery's solved. That's why I've never been here."

The car stopped and she scrambled out of it, not willing to wait for Ajax or his driver to open the door. The further away the wedding got, the weirder she felt in her dress. The edgier she felt in general.

Every time he'd kissed her, the fog of fantasy had closed in around them and it had seemed a dream. Now, standing in front of his glass-and-steel house, the sun's harsh light bathing her skin in heat, the breeze coming up from the sea blowing the skirt of her wedding dress around her ankles, it all felt much too real.

"Can we go inside?" she asked. "I'm overheated."

"As you would be in that dress." He led the way to the house, and she followed, relief washing through her when they entered the cool stone foyer.

"Are you all right now?"

"Better, thank you." She folded her hands and put them in front of her, the folds of her skirt hiding them.

"Hopefully your things will be here soon. I imagine that is quite uncomfortable."

She looked down and took a breath at the same time, her breasts trying to escape the bodice. Again.

Her things. Because she was expected to live here. To drop everything for this. For him. Because he wanted it to look real.

"So," she said, her voice tight, her next words escaping before she had the chance to think them through, fueled by her nerves, by her need to know what he was thinking. What he might ask of her. "Are we about to consummate this marriage?"

"What?"

"You said...you said you were so eager to consummate, and you're having my things sent here. You want to get on that?"

"I think not," he said, dark brows drawn together, his grasp of her sarcasm clearly loose at best. "Certainly not tonight."

"What exactly is the marriage going to be? And if not tonight, do you see it happening in the future?"

"I wanted to present a certain front to the press. That's all. Per the agreement we signed this afternoon, we have to stay married for five years before the deal is finalized, or ownership of the company defaults to..."

"It would go to Alex, wouldn't it?"

"Considering your father's health? And if he stays with your sister that long? Likely. That means whatever happens, this marriage is not going to be quick and easy. Even then... even then perhaps it would be best for us to consider making this arrangement permanent. However, you have just stepped in at the last minute—I'm hardly going to force you upstairs to ravish you."

Her breath caught in her throat. "That's not what I..."

"You were the one who asked," he said.

"Just making things clear. We *did* get married today, and you did make a comment about consummation," she threw back.

"So you're offering me your body, as well? Right now? How about here? I could dismiss my staff, or hell, they're paid to look the other way, why bother dismissing them? Would you like me to tear your dress off and have you against the wall?"

His voice was rough, unsteady, like nothing she'd heard from him before.

She'd pushed him to a place she hadn't intended, the conversation not seeming as absurd as she'd imagined when she'd first spoken the words. There was an edge of danger, reality to all of this. She'd never seen him like this. This close to losing grip on his control.

Being in the path of it was almost frightening. But she was close to the edge, too. She felt vulnerable and at a disadvantage, two things she hated. And pushing at his control made her feel like she had even more of it.

"I could, Leah. Some women like that. Or, if you prefer I could take you upstairs and make you my wife for real. But the thing is, I would be doing it because I'm angry. At her. I would think of her. She is the only woman I have ever loved, and she walked away from me on our wedding day to be with someone else. Someone I despise. If I were with you," he continued, his voice rough, "it would be to get back at her. I'm a man—never forget that. I could think of anything and get it up while I parted your thighs. It would hardly make you special. Yes, I could have you. But the question is, right now, would you want me?"

His words shouldn't hurt. But they were so cold, so hard, they cut through her defenses, straight to her heart.

But she wouldn't let him see.

"You loved her?" she asked.

"I *love* her," he said. "Years of loving someone isn't erased by one act. As convenient as it might be."

"I suppose not."

The whole thing made her pride burn. How adamant he was about not wanting her. And at the same time, she looked into his dark eyes and realized his own pride was savaged. Realized how hard this was for him.

He'd lost the woman he loved. He had married someone else. Someone he had no feelings for. He was looking at her and seeing a broken dream. No matter how strong her armor, she felt the impact of that like a battering ram against the steel.

"I think I'll go to my room then, since you're not interested in a quick consummation," she said, her tone tart, her expression as neutral as she could get it. "Good night."

He nodded once. "Tomorrow, we'll come up with a plan."

"I look forward to it."

Maybe a night of sleep would help her figure out what she was doing. Help her figure out what had happened to her.

And what they were going to do about it.

CHAPTER THREE

AJAX WOKE UP without a hangover. Because he hadn't been able to bring himself to drink. As Leah had observed, he didn't drink alcohol. He prized his control far too much. Vice was the downfall of man.

The need for a certain high, whether it be from alcohol, drugs or sex was responsible for much of the evil in the world. Something he'd lived at one point in time. Something he'd witnessed in horrific detail. And something he'd done his best to destroy, even if it was only one small piece of it.

He did not let vice own him. Not anymore. He didn't even give it a foothold on his soul.

Rachel leaving wasn't reason enough to give that up. But, *Theos,* it burned his pride. He hadn't imagined pride had such a place in his life, but apparently it did.

He stalked down the stairs, wearing nothing but a pair of black pants, not bothering to get dressed. He was not in the mood to deal with much of anything or anyone.

He stalked through the house and into the dining room, where the one thing he couldn't avoid dealing with was sitting, perched on the edge of a chair, a cup of coffee in her hands, her whiskey-colored eyes round. She looked very like a lost child. And he had no patience to deal with it. Any of it.

"I trust you slept well?" he asked, attempting civility because regardless of his feelings it was the appropriate way to treat one's wife. Or so he imagined.

"Not in the least," she returned, her voice crisp.

Her dark, curly hair was tied up, a little puffball on top of her head, and she was wearing a baggy sweater, the sort that made generous breasts blend into a woman's waist, concealing any nice attributes her figure might possess.

Not that he cared. Her figure was the least of his concerns.

"If the mattress is a problem for you, a new one can be ordered."

"I don't think it was the mattress so much as the unexpected acquisition of a husband, but I could be wrong. Maybe the sleep surface was too firm."

"You seem a bit off this morning."

Her fingers flexed around the cup, giving the impression of claws. "Do I?"

He found he wanted to push her. He was spoiling for a fight and he couldn't say why. He'd never tried to pick a fight for no reason in his life. He'd grown up in such a volatile environment, and he'd learned early on that the quickest way to an early death, or at the very least a world of pain, was to cause trouble.

Keeping his head down, doing as he was told, all while planning, planning and strategizing, finding a way out—that was the way to survive.

Today, he didn't just want to survive. He wanted to fight. It seemed a perfect substitute for getting drunk.

"Hardly the blushing bride," he said. "You look like hell, to be honest."

"Are you always such an ass?"

Good. She was getting angry. That was what he wanted. What he craved right now.

"Perhaps you've never had the chance to really get to know me before now, though, in the interest of full disclosure, I am in a bloody bad mood this morning."

"I'm glad to know this at least qualifies as a bad mood. Why are you taking it out on me?"

He didn't know. He didn't know why his control was fraying. Why he wasn't being self-contained. Why he was suddenly incapable of maintaining an iron grip on emotion. "Because you're here, *agape mou*. The lucky replacement bride."

"Would my sister be on the receiving end of this treatment? If so, I can certainly see why she ran out on the wedding."

"If your sister were here, I daresay we might still be in bed. And I would certainly be in a better mood."

Something flashed in her amber eyes that he didn't like. Pain? He had gone a step too far in venting his anger. Saying things he wasn't even certain he felt just to simply let the anger continue. Indulging emotion for once rather than sublimating it.

He didn't know how sleeping with Rachel would make him feel. The idea of it…it had made him tense. But that was to be expected, considering the nature of their relationship, and everything else.

But sex with his wife was half the appeal of marriage to him. Everything in life had a place. A fire burning in the fireplace was all well and good. But when the fire spread outside of it, that became a problem.

Yes, things had their place. And he had been looking forward to having everything where it was meant to be.

But now the plan was upended. And he wasn't certain of his next move. For a man who liked to plan ahead, it was disconcerting at best.

"I am sorry," he bit out. "That was crass of me. I'm frustrated, and it has very little to do with you personally." Except, somehow, the frustration, or rather, his inability to manage it, did seem tied to her.

She blinked, and he could see some of the tension release from her body. "Of course not. Of course. None of this really has anything to do with me personally, does it?"

"I'm glad you have such a good grasp on the situation."

"I don't, Ajax, not even close. What, if you'll excuse me, in hell do you want from me? Do you want me to just hang out for the next five years, living in your house, and then go on my merry way like none of this ever happened?"

"Clearly that cannot happen," he said.

"Clearly?"

"I would not disrespect you that way."

"Oh, honey, after all the crap you said to me last night, you're saying you don't want to disrespect me?"

"I was angry."

"Great. So was I. So am I."

"I apologized."

"An apology isn't a magic healing potion, it's just a bandage. It covered up some of my pique nicely, but it's hardly healed."

"Well," he said, shifting his weight to the balls of his feet, "perhaps we can set it aside in the interest of figuring out what it is we need to do?"

"All right," she said.

"We're married, and we really had no other choice, all things considered."

"Yes."

"And we have to stay married for at least five years."

"Uh-huh," she said.

"And I planned on marrying into your family. On keeping Holt in your family. I want to be married. I would like to have children. A real marriage suits me."

"Oh, indeed?"

"Yes. I wanted a wife. A wife was always my end goal."

"Except she was tall, blond, a size four and named Rachel?"

"Yes," he said, teeth gritted. "But in the end, what difference does it make?"

"Is that really how you feel? Do I matter that little… Does she?"

"It isn't you, Leah. I have had a plan for my life from the moment I left my father's house. I planned to work my way up, and I did. To make a new start for myself with nothing but hard work, honesty. To never, ever set foot back on the path

I was born to walk. And I have done that. I met your family, and your father and mother made me feel welcomed. Like a son. And then there was Rachel. Everything fit. It all seemed perfect. I knew the first time I saw her she was my end goal. That she would be my wife. She is the first part of my plan that has dared not to fall into place."

"Yes, well, that's because she's a woman and not a business venture."

"But we would have been perfect," he said.

"No, Ajax, you wouldn't have been. You would have been fine, but not perfect. Because she's not perfect. *You* certainly aren't."

"But it made sense," he said. "In my head...in my head she made everything fall into place."

"She's not a business venture, and she's not an ideal, either."

He rubbed his temples with his fingertips. "I know that."

"Well, you don't seem to. You talk like marriage to her was your end goal and then...and then what? It would just be perfect? Your life would suddenly be perfect?"

"I can't... It's hard to... I've been working, Leah, so hard, all of my life. I came to your family's home, and your parents treated me more like a son than an employee. They took me in, gave me focus and purpose. Your father set me on this path. He taught me things, taught me how to be a man, to be strong. He gave me goals. He sent me to school. I have been walking that path he set me on, tirelessly, never looking away from the goal, from the end."

"To where you would make Holt continue on for him. Where you would be part of our family."

"I've been walking for a long time," he said.

"And then you reach the end and you rest?"

"And then maybe I don't have to work so hard to stay in control all the damn time because I'll have arrived at a more stable point," he bit out. "My...everything would be in place."

Because things weren't now. He'd made money, obtained

power and connections. He'd used all of the resources at his disposal to bring down his father's drug and human trafficking ring. And he still couldn't rest. He still didn't feel he could stop working. Stop trying to distance himself from his past.

From all he had done.

"Why do you need to hang on to control so tightly, Ajax?" she asked, her eyes filled with...sympathy. Pity. If she knew who she was talking to, if she knew the beast that lived inside him, she wouldn't look at him like that.

He stood and started to pace the room. "It's nothing. This is nothing. It can still be fixed."

Leah studied him, noticed the tension in his jaw, in the lines of his body. He was uncomfortable, and thrown off. And she had to take into account that he could very well be heartbroken.

He said he loved Rachel. But for the first time she wondered. Wondered if he'd ever known her really, or if she'd just been symbolic for him.

"I have a plan, Leah," he said.

She crossed her arms beneath her breasts. "Oh, good. Let's hear it."

He stopped moving, his hands locked behind his back. "First, we must show a united front. I am taking over a massive corporation here, changing the layout in some respects. We need to show solidarity—I will not appear weak."

"No, you wouldn't." She couldn't imagine him appearing weak anyway.

"And I will not be seen as a man forced into this situation."

"Pride is a beautiful thing. At least I think it is. I don't know that I have any left."

"I find myself in short supply, as well." His expression turned fierce. "And I will turn my focus to helping mass produce Leah's Lollies products, as soon as time allows."

She ignored the leap her heart took and looked down at her fingernails. "Payment for services rendered?"

He looked stricken for a moment, and his face paled. Then,

as soon as the reaction occurred, he covered it again. "This is not that sort of arrangement. You are my wife. Not a woman I have purchased."

"And how long will I be your wife?" That was the one bit left undiscussed. Undecided. Would she be his wife on paper, or in reality.

"I made vows," he said. "I intend to honor them. Do you?"

"In what regard?"

"In all regards. What's the sense in divorce when this union could serve us both?"

"We're missing the love bit."

"You don't strike me as the kind of woman who's overly romantic."

He was right. Now. It hadn't always been true. But over time…over time all that sunny optimism had bled from her, an open vein that had truly begun the hemorrhage the moment she'd first seen Rachel standing by Ajax. The perfect couple, so beautiful, so poised. The embodiment of her heartbreak.

"I'm not especially. But what do I get out of this, Ajax? Beyond a husband who is bitter toward me and will think of other women if we ever make love?"

He looked her over, slowly, and something changed in his eyes, heat sparking in their dark depths. Heat that lit an answering fire in her stomach. Heat that reminded her just how strong a pull Ajax had over body.

"What do I get?" she repeated, her voice a whisper.

"What do you want?"

As they'd both pointed out, their pride was all but destroyed. So why cling to it now? She wasn't going to sit around, angry over not getting what she wanted because she hadn't asked for it. She was going to make her own demands. If he wanted a marriage, she would give him a marriage.

She had her armor now—she didn't need love. She didn't want it. Didn't want emotion. But a business partnership, cemented by marriage, that she could handle. And sex with Ajax?

Well, she was attracted to him. And frankly, she was over being a virgin. This was a convenient way to deal with both her attraction to him and the virginity. A win-win situation, really.

And yeah, kissing him had knocked her defenses a bit, but it wouldn't happen again. Not when she was the one making demands. Not when it was expected.

She would make this a marriage that would work for her, not just for him. To hell with his plans, she had plans of her own. If he said no, maybe he'd release her.

But if he said yes…

"If we're going to stay married, then I want a marriage. I want you, in my bed, every night, and never with another woman. I want you to support me personally and professionally. I won't live a half life forever because of a rash decision I made."

"Naturally," he said, "I want children, as I said already. It has always been a part of my plan. And you?"

She hadn't given it a lot of thought, because marriage had seemed a far-off event. But part of her had always taken for granted that she would be a mother someday.

"I want them," she said, trying not to think too deeply about it.

"And as you are my wife, sleeping with you seems only logical. What is the point of seeking physical release elsewhere?"

"I'm relieved you feel that way." Though not overly flattered. "Better for our health, wellness and media image, I imagine."

"However, I stand by my original statement. You and I may figure out the finer points of our relationship after this whole thing has been smoothed over in the public arena. While we're attending events as blissful newlyweds, it would be best if our personal relationship was kept as simple as possible. I don't want Christofides thinking there might be a weakness he can exploit. I don't want him to get desperate and decide he should come and seduce you."

"Me?"

"He may very well if he sees that Rachel is a dead end to destroying my goals."

"Oh, seduced for revenge from my marriage that's for business only. I am such a lucky girl."

"It's the reality, Leah. I don't say it to insult."

"Of course not."

"Also in favor of waiting, you need time to adjust."

"Time to adjust? What do you... What?"

"Yesterday you were to be my sister-in-law—today, you're my wife, I doubt you're prepared for the change. In spite of what I said about you not being a prisoner, and while I know you entered into the arrangement of your own free will, it was an emotionally heightened moment, and there were a lot of reasons why our marriage made sense in terms of business. But just because all of that made sense, does not mean you and I make sense as a couple. Naturally, you will need time before you're ready to consummate."

She blinked, unable to wrap her mind around what he'd just said. "Need...time?"

"Naturally."

She felt raw. Her ego wounded and scrubbed with salt. And now he was telling her what she wanted. To hell with that. "You have no idea what I'm ready for, what I want. Don't you dare think you can tell me. I'm quite okay with sex, the idea of us having sex sits very well with me. I didn't agree to marry you thoughtlessly, I know what being married means."

"You're young, Leah, naive. I will not take advantage of that. A little time for everyone to adjust to the situation is necessary."

She felt defiant now, her pride, that pride she'd decided only a moment ago she didn't care much about. "I don't need time, Ajax. You could have me on this table right now if you want. Think of my sister. Hell, think of England, I don't care. I know what I want. I said exactly what I wanted. I want you."

The words hung, heavy in the silence of the room. She'd admitted it. That she wanted him. That she wanted to sleep with him. Something about the admission made her feel stronger. Made her feel like her armor was back in place.

"The thing is," he said, his voice a growl, "I don't want you. You are a child to me. I look at you and I see a girl. I do not see a woman."

His words didn't hurt as badly as they might have, not with her armor on. Not when she could see, so easily, that he was lashing out because of pain in him. Not because of her. "I'm twenty-three. I am not a child."

The anger in his eyes dissipated, and he just looked tired. "I...I have not had time to adjust to the new plan."

Just then she found it hard to be mad at him, in spite of the cutting edge to his words. "And the plan is everything, right?" A new thing she'd learned about him in the past twenty-four hours.

"Yes, Leah, the plan is damn well everything," he said, each syllable rough and hard. "How do you navigate life without one?"

"Follow your heart. Your passions..."

"Passion," he spat, as though the word tasted terrible on his tongue, "is the single most destructive element in life I can think of."

"You don't feel passion?"

"I deny it."

"Not even for Rachel?"

He shook his head, dark eyes blank. "For nothing. For no one."

"I thought you loved her."

"What does that have to do with passion?" he asked.

"Everything."

He shook his head. "That's where you're wrong, Leah. Passion is all about self. All about pleasing yourself. And that path...that path can get very dark."

And then Ajax turned and walked out of the room, and the last bit of fantasy and mist that had hung before her eyes evaporated.

There was nothing more than cold reality and the realization that the man she'd thought she'd known for most of her life was nothing more than a stranger.

CHAPTER FOUR

AJAX NEEDED A new plan. All things considered, the plan wasn't as derailed as it seemed at first. He was still married to a Holt heiress, and he still possessed Holt Enterprises. He had a wife, albeit not the wife he'd wanted, but from that wife he would still get the children he needed to continue on his legacy. A legacy he had reason to feel proud of. In theory.

As for Rachel…his feelings for her were not essential to the plan. Love, however nice it had been as an idea, was not essential to the plan.

As far as the sex went…it had been Rachel in his mind for so long, it was hard to transfer the desire to Leah. Leah, who was ten years his junior. Leah, who had so much softness in her. At least, she'd had it in her. Back when they used to talk, she'd been so open. She'd connected with him on a level that was so different from anyone else. But in terms of wanting her? That could wait. Until he'd got used to the idea at least.

Sex was, by the account of some, a basic human need, much like eating and drinking.

He disagreed. He'd done well without it for more years than he cared to recall. Just as he'd never needed alcohol. He valued control over all else, and anything that might distract him had been weeded out as unnecessary. That said, he couldn't lie. He'd been looking forward to that part of marriage.

The acknowledgment of it nearly made him laugh. He liked

to think of himself as being entirely above desire, but that wasn't the case. He was simply very good at keeping it on a leash. The hours he spent working out late at night were a testament to the fact that he was sublimating desire, rather than absent of it completely.

Leah was his wife. His real wife, per the new plan outlined this morning.

He repeated that, over and over in his mind, trying to make it real. Trying to incorporate it into his vision for the future. Trying to figure out where she fit in with his end goal.

There was a fund-raiser tonight, for one of Ajax's favored charities and that meant that the personal things would have to go on hold for a moment. He would worry about the physical piece of the marriage later. For tonight, they would simply have to put on a show for the people and press attending the fund-raiser.

He closed his thoughts down, narrowed his focus. He walked through the house, his footsteps loud on the tile. He hadn't seen Leah since their argument that morning.

He finally found her in the study, her laptop on her lap, dark hair piled on her head. She'd ditched the baggy sweatshirt in favor of a T-shirt and yoga pants. She had a pen in her mouth, four bags of candy in front of her, with the highly recognizable pink-and-green-polka-dot logo associated with Leah's Lollies, and she was typing furiously.

"I see your things arrived."

She paused and looked up, golden eyes round. Then she straightened and tugged the pen from between her lips. "Yeah, and I had a few issues to deal with."

"Chocolate emergency?"

"You'd be surprised. Some quality control stuff. I had to go and grab a few random bags of product to run an unofficial check. I haven't found any problems, but I guess some deformed butterscotch high heels went through to the boutiques.

I'm not very thrilled about it. Actually, Holt is my manufacturer, you know. I pay them, it's all aboveboard, not a nepotism thing."

"So you're a client in addition to the Holt Corporation holding shares."

"Indeed."

"But now you've married into part ownership of Holt. I would suppose that means the shares are passing back to you in many ways. And now you own more of Leah's Lollies."

"One of my wins. One of the very few."

"Perhaps few in this situation, but in general, it seems you've had quite a few. This is what you always said you wanted. You were always telling me about your ideas for a store. Pink, you said. It would be pink. Now they make paint that comes in Leah Pink, don't they?"

She cocked her head to the side, a line creasing her forehead. "How did you know that?"

"I read about your work." If there was a news article about her on a website, he clicked it, naturally. And occasionally, he was enticed to do an internet search to see how things were doing. Because it was nice to see how things were going for her. Because she was Rachel's sister. It was only natural.

"Oh. Huh." She looked back down at her screen, then back up. "Sorry, did you need something?"

"I forgot to mention that there is a charity event tonight Rachel and I planned on attending. Given the circumstances surrounding our marriage I'm certain the media will be there, and they will be waiting for the story."

"You mean…we have to go to this?"

"Yes. If we miss it…if we miss it we're inviting speculation. I will not give that to the public. I'll not give it to Christofides."

She put her hand on her forehead. "Oh, jeez."

"Yes. Have you got a gown?"

"I have several. It's a bad habit of mine, buying dresses that

I don't really have any reason to wear. Don't judge. Everyone needs a hobby."

"Well, in this case it seems it's served us both well."

"I suppose."

He looked at her, and more specifically, at the way she wasn't looking at him. Not really. Not the way she usually did. Usually when he looked at her, he saw the girl with sparkling eyes.

She looked different now. No glitter. Her face a bit more drawn, sculpted. And she seemed tired. He'd never seen her looking tired before. Leah was a woman of endless energy, at least she'd always seemed so to him. A constant sugar high that never seemed to end.

But it had ended sometime. She was so much harder now, but he hadn't seen it till the past twenty-four hours.

"You will need to be ready by six."

"Okay," she said, not looking back up at him.

"And you will need to not look like you're contemplating putting my head on a pike."

"No guarantees, darling," she said, her words carrying a razor-sharp edge.

"We're supposed to be newlyweds."

"We *are* newlyweds. Marriage is hard. First twelve hours is the hardest." She continued typing away, not looking at him.

"So it seems. But we must attempt to make this look real."

"It is real. As you pointed out, I signed a license, I took vows. It's all real, man."

"You know what I mean."

"Love," she said, looking up at him. "You want it to look like love. You want me to gaze at you in adoration so no one doubts my happiness or your penis size—I got it."

His throat tightened, a strange kind of heat prickling his face. "You do not normally talk this way."

"Maybe I do, Ajax…how would you know? When was the

last time we had a real conversation? Six years ago? We don't know each other. I didn't think you were as big of a jerk as you played it this morning, but hey, I learned something new. And you think I'm a child, but you're wrong about that, too. We're learning new things. What do you know about that?"

"I think you're having a fit because you're angry at me."

She shot him a deadly glare. "Fits are what little girls have. I'm a woman, I'm in a mood."

"Is that it, then? I'm not accustomed to dealing with women and their moods."

"And why is that?"

"Because I'm not accustomed to living with a woman. When a woman is in a mood, I am able to avoid her."

"Oh, how charming. You only deal with them when they're all sweet for you."

"That is not it. I was not being insulting, I was making an observation."

"Oh." She looked down again. "Well, anyway... Look, I get that tonight is a big deal. I don't want to screw it up, either. I'm already being called the backup bride by the press, and I'm not all that enamored with the title so it suits me just fine if everyone thinks we've fallen into a mad passionate affair."

"That is part of the plan. My plan."

"The new plan?"

"We did need one."

"You know...everyone will think that we betrayed Rachel."

"Will they?"

"With a bride switch two hours before the wedding? It's either she betrayed you or you betrayed her."

"Betrayal doesn't need to come into it. What if we realized we really loved each other, while Rachel and I were merely marrying for convenience?"

Leah felt like she was being stabbed in the heart, slowly, each new inch he pushed the blade in burning fresh like a new cut. And she didn't know why it hurt. Why, after managing as well as she had with every other slight, this went so deep.

It was nothing to do with Ajax specifically, but with coming in second to Rachel again. Every boy she'd ever dated had nearly got whiplash watching Rachel walk by. And Ajax…Ajax had preferred her, too.

Her mother and father had always loved them both, and treated them both well, but Rachel had an ease about her. An elegance that people responded to instantly. She was beautiful, poised, long and lean.

Leah had always been awkward by comparison. Her life had not been the social whirlwind Rachel's had been, not ever. There had never been too many party invites, or lots of cute boys. She was the Other Holt. She was the incidental, the afterthought. And that realization always hurt, no matter how many layers of armor she put between herself and the world.

"Do you think people will buy it?"

"Why not?" he asked, shrugging.

"What about what Rachel might say?"

"It's Christofides I worry about. What has she told him? And what might he entice her to say?"

"Oh. Yes. That's right. The evil boyfriend of doom."

"Perhaps one of us should…"

"Me," she said. The idea of Ajax calling Rachel was a bit much to handle. "I'll do it." She closed the laptop and stood, tucking her computer under her arm, ignoring the slight awkwardness of the position. "And then I'll…get ready for tonight."

"Okay."

"Great."

Something changed in his expression, a strange look in his eyes. "Tell her…tell her I said hi."

She clutched the computer more tightly to her body, and tried to ignore the strange wave of sadness that crested and crashed over her. For him. For her. "I will."

* * *

She shut the door to her new room behind her and took her phone from her bedside table. She clicked on the text her sister had sent yesterday and hit reply.

You ok?

She paced, the phone in her hand, and when it buzzed, she jumped a little before looking at the screen.

I'm good. Is Jax ok?

Her sister's nickname for Ajax always made Leah bristle a little. Perhaps because it was a reminder of their special relationship.

He's ok. Leah sucked in a sharp breath and typed the rest of the message. He married me, BTW.

She winced and hit Send. Then waited. Her sister's response came quickly.

Holy crap. Just saw it on Google.

Leah waited for more. For anything, but there was nothing. So she started a new message.

You're happy? You didn't love Ajax did you?

Her phone pinged.

Not like that. Not the kind you need to marry a guy. You know?

Do you love Alex? Leah sent the message.

The reply took longer than the ones before. I need to be with Alex.

No declarations of love. Or even of happiness. It made Leah feel heavy

You're really okay?

I'm tougher than you think.

If anyone asks—Leah stopped typing and thought for a second before continuing—tell them that you and Ajax were marrying for the company. Tell them we fell in love and you let us get married.

Why?

Leah blew out an exasperated breath.

For his pride.

Tell him I am sorry. And I'll tell the press and curious people whatever you want. I have my own problems to deal with.

I'll tell him. And he says hi. She hit Send on it before she could delete the last part. She almost wanted to. Almost wanted to hide that bit of his vulnerability.

Thanks. I don't know when I'll be back. There are things that I need to take care of. I love you.

Leah sighed. Me too.

Leah threw her phone down onto the bed and let out a long growl. She noticed her sister did not return Ajax's hi. Which she found annoying, for no good reason. She was trapped between feeling protective of him and feeling angry at him, and somewhere between that, she was just mad for herself. Upset about the entire situation.

Well, there was no time for that. It didn't matter how she

felt, not right now. She took a deep breath and stalked over to her closet, which had been all arranged for her over the course of the day by Ajax's very helpful staff.

Nope. No sulking allowed. She had a dress to choose, and she had to look appropriately amazing. She had to get her mask on. Because no matter the story, she was still going to be Ajax Kouros's backup bride.

Because it was going to be a high school flashback all over again. Instead of *Who Wore it Better?* It would be *Who Hung on Ajax's Arm Better?*

Hmph. She was done with this.

If she had anything to do with it, she would be Ajax Kouros's fabulously sexy backup bride, who didn't flinch against the flashbulbs, or the comparisons. She only hoped her defenses held.

CHAPTER FIVE

THE WOMAN WHO walked downstairs to greet him that night was an entirely different woman from the one who had been on the couch in the study earlier.

Frizzy, mahogany curls had been tamed into softer waves, whiskey-colored eyes were lined with dark makeup, making them glow. And unlike her T-shirt and sweatpants, her black dress didn't hang off her curves. The one-shouldered, Grecian-inspired gown molded to her curves, revealing no skin but giving everyone an insight into the figure beneath.

Her lips were painted cherry-red, the perfect accent to a showstopping ensemble. She was playing her part well. She looked every inch the woman in love, the woman trying to appeal to her new husband.

It wasn't just the clothes that made her seem different. It was the way she looked at him. Or rather it was the way she didn't look at him. Her chin was tilted up, her expression cool. Haughty. Always Leah Holt had looked at him with a special glitter in her eyes. No one else had ever looked at him that way. No one else had ever smiled at him as she had, with open affection and warmth. No one else had ever left chocolate on his desk, just because.

He'd lost that somewhere along the way. And it wasn't until now that he missed it.

"You look beautiful," he said. It was true. She did. He realized the truth of it as he spoke it. He'd always put up a block where Leah was concerned. She was too young for him to look at her like that.

And he had been looking at one woman for years, a woman who was wholly different in looks and personality, and it was not an immediate thing, to want to look at anyone else.

Though Leah's transformation was startling enough that he had to look, was powerless to do anything else.

Startling, not necessarily welcome. It seemed to him that the chill emanating from her like mist over frost would be obvious to anyone who saw them.

And then she smiled, red lips parting, and he could see how false it was.

"Let's go then," she said, extending her arm.

He took it, drawing her close to his side and leading her out the front door where the car was already waiting.

She leaned into her step, her body coming into fuller contact with his. He paused, and for a full second, he was unable to look away from the lush outline of her breasts. Fire kicked through him, a quick burst of it, like kerosene being thrown on a match. It was like nothing he'd felt for years. Nothing he'd let himself feel.

Nothing he'd felt since he was a boy. Surrounded by all of the women he could have. No one to tell him no. Until…

He let out the breath he hadn't realized he'd been holding. No. He wouldn't think of that. He wouldn't look at her that way.

He gritted his teeth and moved away from her, rounding the car to open her door for her before going to the driver's side and getting in.

They might have been a couple who'd been married for years. They were comfortably silent on the ride, Leah keeping her eyes on her phone while he kept his eyes on the road, taking the time to enjoy the way his car handled the turns.

It was one of his few indulgences. Cars. He liked different cars. The way they handled, the rate at which they accelerated. Driving was the one time he could keep a blank mind. The one time he could loosen his focus on the plan and simply see what was in front of him.

He was almost feeling relaxed by the time they pulled up to the front of the hotel where the event was being held. This could work. This sort of side-by-side existence.

It was only when he got out of the car and rounded to her side, when the flashbulbs started going off, and when he reached in and took her hand, helping her out, when he saw the frost in her eyes, that he felt the ease slip.

The blast of light from the camera revealed a flatness in her gaze. And tomorrow everyone would see it. They would have to be blind to miss it.

It took him a moment to realize she was smiling. Because he had only been looking at her eyes. And there was no smile there.

"Ready, darling husband?" she asked, the brittle steel in her voice carrying over to her posture, her body rigid, tense.

"Ready, *agape mou*." He slid his arm around her waist, pulled her up against the side of his body. He'd held her close yesterday, kissed her lips. But then he'd been high on adrenaline, completely disconnected from his body. He'd been focused only on one thing: getting out of the wedding venue before questions had started pouring in.

And he'd succeeded. But there had been no time then, to think of her lips, of her curves, how soft and warm she felt up against him.

Suddenly it was the only thing he could think about. From shouting at her this morning, to the wave of lust he was battling with tonight, Leah seemed to make a mockery of his control.

Marriage had been intended to make everything easier, but so far, his was just making things more difficult. Made him feel like he was being dragged backward. Back to the place he'd started. Back to the man he'd been.

Back into hell. Where he wasn't one of those suffering eternal damnation, no. That would be too kind. In his hell, he was the one meting it out.

He closed his eyes for a moment, blocking out the camera flashes. Blocking out the memories.

He led her up the steps and into the hotel, all the while smiling, at her, not at the photographers. It would look much better in the photos. Make a better headline.

He would close it off. The desire. The heat. He moved his fingers, gently, over the indent of her waist. He was used to going places with Rachel like this, with his arm around her like this. But Leah was different. Her waist nipped in a bit more, her hips flaring out wider, where Rachel was flat and slender.

An observation, that was all. And yet he did find it interesting. He moved his hand down slightly, to the rounded curve of her hip. Yes, very interesting.

"Do you have to do that?" she said, her voice choked.

"Do what?"

"Touch me like that?"

"You are my wife. And if I'm not remembering wrongly, you told me yesterday that you wanted me in your bed. Every night. In light of that I should not think my hand on your clothed body would be an issue."

"I didn't think we were worrying about our personal relationship until after we got our public one under control."

"This is our public relationship, *agape.*"

"Sorry," she said. "Felt like personal territory."

"And it disturbs you?" he asked. God knew it disturbed him. This entire change in her physical appearance disturbed him. She wasn't conforming to the box he'd put her into, and he didn't like it in the least.

They passed through the double doors that led to the glittering antechamber of the hotel ballroom. The white marble floor was edged in black, the design echoed on the walls. White pillars were stationed throughout, a nod, albeit a highly glossed one, to an ancient Grecian temple.

"Yes. No. I don't know."

"You are prepared to sleep with me and yet personal disturbs you?"

"Will you stop bringing that up?" she hissed. "This is not about our personal lives. This is our public life, right?" She smiled at a passing photographer.

"Unless our personal life starts to affect the public facade, which was the entire point of us leaving it as it is for now."

"I don't know, seems like it was never the best idea. I'm not sure our personal life is all that great."

"I'm not sure we have one."

He felt her go stiff beneath his touch. "No. I daresay that is what you'd think." Her words were as stilted as her posture. "After all, I've never been to your house. When you practically grew up living in mine."

"Your father's."

"How many Christmas parties have you been to at my penthouse in New York?" she asked.

"A few," he said.

"Yes, and yet I had never been to your house once until yesterday. So of course you don't think we have a personal relationship. I guess I'm the one who thought we did. The one who thought we at least had respect between us. I won't be so stupid again." She pulled a glass of champagne off the tray of a passing waiter and took a few fortifying sips.

A couple of businessmen stopped them and started talking about the new acquisition of Holt with an enthusiasm that only those in the acquire and assimilate game could convey over that kind of topic.

Normally, Leah would have got in on the conversation. She was interested in business and particularly in Holt. Right now though, all she could really do was nod along while she forced champagne down her throat. A delicate balance. Don't drink too much, inhibitions might lower. But a certain amount was required to weather something like this.

She knew this game, this game of putting on armor. Playing polished and playing tough. But things were slipping when she was with him. And it sucked. Old feelings were getting stirred up, getting a second life thanks to all of the close proximity. And she didn't want that.

I want you. In my bed, every night.

Yes, she'd really said that to him.

She kept on smiling. Why was she doing this now? Why was she breaking down now? With him on her arm and people all around them?

She sucked in a breath and held it. She was fine. She would be fine. She'd spent her life proving herself. She hadn't excelled in school, but she'd been able to shine in business, and shine she had. No, she wasn't the most beautiful Holt heiress, but she had her own charisma. And she had business savvy. And she'd done whatever was necessary to get herself to the point where the media no longer called her an ugly duckling, but a socialite turned businesswoman.

She hadn't done those things by being sweet and open and leaving candy on people's desks. She'd changed. She'd learned to protect herself. And she would keep on doing that.

But she *would* have him. Because she wanted him. Because there had to be a perk to being trapped in this marriage with him, and if access to his body was the perk? She was more than happy with that.

Yes. She was. Indeed.

It wasn't about emotions. It wasn't about the ache in her chest that had shown up the day before the wedding and had insisted on sticking around.

Sex wouldn't hurt. It would feel good. At least, she imagined it would.

It was probably best they were waiting. She needed to get hold of her virginal nerves and beat them into submission. She'd shown him enough of her vulnerability when she'd been a lovelorn teenager. No, he didn't get any more. She was *taking* now.

So there.

The men, who had been droning all through her drinking and nodding along and fake smiling at whoever passed, were done now and were headed away from them. She was pretty sure she'd forgotten to say goodbye, but she'd been too lost in her own thoughts.

"So what now?" she asked. "Make more small talk? Smile for the camera? Do a dance for all of our admirers?" She gestured out toward the dance floor.

"I don't dance," he said, straightening his shoulders.

Just looking at him hurt. He was the epitome of masculine beauty in his tux, dark hair short and neat, not a hair out of place. And yet, there was something about him, no matter how contained he looked, that hinted at something darker beneath the surface. Something frozen in a block of ice. All it would take was a little heat and…

"We should dance," she said, lifting her chin, feeling defiant. Feeling angry. At herself mostly, for being such a stupid… girl where he was concerned. A look at his powerful physique and she got all fluttery. If he flashed ab she'd probably die.

Pathetic, woman. Pathetic.

"I already told you," he said, his voice hushed, "I don't…"

"But I do. And you deprived me of a dance on our wedding day since you were so eager to have me alone." She arched a brow. "You wouldn't deny your bride her first dance with her husband, would you?"

Something, she didn't know what, compelled her to push further, harder. Maybe it was the fact that he was acting like the wounded party. Like this wasn't a major deal for her. Like it was okay to just turn her down in front of all these people. She took a step toward him, placed her palm flat against his chest.

He didn't feel like ice. No, not even close. He was fire

against her skin, and with very little trouble she knew he could melt her.

"Dance with me," she whispered, keeping her eyes trained on his.

He caught her wrist, a strange look in his eye, one of curiosity. Detached, but present. He bent his head, his eyes never leaving hers, and lifted her arm to his lips, pressing a kiss to the sensitive underside of her wrist.

It sent a shiver over her veins, back to her heart, which jolted in response. Her stomach tightened to the point of pain, breathing a luxury her body couldn't afford. Not at the moment, not when all of her was focused on Ajax's lips against her bare skin.

"I think it would be best if I waited to hold you like that until we're in private," he said, his tone intimate, husky, and yet, she was aware of the people that were standing close, potentially overhearing. "I do not trust myself where you're concerned."

Everything in her shook. Breathing becoming impossible. "All right then," she said, her voice a choked whisper. More weakness. She hated it. "But you'd better make it very worth my while when we're in private. Don't make promises you can't back up."

"Never, *agape*. Never."

The evening wound down with more small talk, more champagne, more little touches that were dissolving her cool by inches.

And by the time they were driving back to his villa, she was just exhausted. Emotionally. Physically. She wasn't sure how she was supposed to endure this…this marriage. Two days in and she was sure she'd aged ten years.

It was tiring to have to cling to her armor so tightly. Over the years it had become a second skin. Effortless to wear. But now? Now it felt like she was clinging to it for dear life.

She closed her eyes and rested her head on the seat as Ajax maneuvered the car out of the city and onto the back roads. She tried to just breathe steadily. She tried the whole way back.

She tried when he pulled the car up to the house and killed the engine. She tried as they walked inside, side by side, not touching at all.

It was dark in the house. She noticed that Ajax kept a minimum of staff, and that they all clocked out at the end of normal workday hours. Dinners were delivered. Ajax seemed to isolate himself as much as possible, and not by accident.

Weird that he'd wanted to get married at all, but then, that was love for you.

It was why she'd sworn off it so long ago.

Feelings. Feelings were stupid. Feelings were awful. She didn't want to think about feelings. Not the emotional kind.

She turned to look at him, and the heat that had been on a low simmer in her blood all night started firing again, anger stoking the flame, sending the simmer into a rolling boil that she could hardly contain.

She curled her hands into fists as they passed through the entryway, both heading toward the stairs and to their separate rooms. And then she stopped.

"Ajax," she said.

He stopped and turned to look at her, and then the world burned down to nothing but him. There was no time to think, to doubt, to worry. None of that stupid, aching emotion. Because this wasn't desire anymore. It was need. The need to gain some control. To make him react.

To make him desire like she did. Because she couldn't stand that he seemed so cool. Couldn't stand that he was so unshaken.

She took a step toward him and planted both her hands on his shoulders, pushing him back against the wall at the same moment she rose up on her tiptoes to capture his lips in a kiss.

He was still for a moment, and then, with a feral growl, his arm came up to wrap around her waist.

Ajax Kouros was not an easy man to shock, and yet, he had been shocked more than once in the past two days. First by his runaway bride, then by his replacement bride, and now, by the kiss she was giving him.

A kiss that seemed to include her entire body. Maybe more than that. Not just skin and flesh, but her very soul.

It wasn't like anything in his experience. It didn't taste like booze and simple lust. It was passion given breath. And for a moment, there was nothing but the heat, the taste of her lips, the softness of her breasts pressed against his chest. And the intensity that fueled each movement.

He held her close to his body, feeling the shape of her, every inch of her, against him. And then, because it seemed right, because it seemed natural, he raised his other hand and slipped his fingers deep into her thick, wavy hair.

It was like silk, sliding through his fingers, tangling around his hand. He made a fist, trapping the strands in his grasp, holding her to him, keeping her from stopping the kiss. Keeping her from moving away.

This was new. A taste of a woman in a way he'd never before experienced.

Sex, applied in the wrong way, was simply another vice. One he didn't indulge, one he didn't even flirt with. Not anymore. Not now.

But this…this was the shot of whiskey he hadn't had on his wedding day. This was every glass of alcohol, every invitation to a hotel room, every line of cocaine he'd ever refused.

In his life, he'd had every sin laid out before him. And there had been a time when he'd indulged himself in them. But there was a point where he had made the choice to turn away. Not because he was a saint, but because in him lived the darkest of tendencies. To embrace temptation. To drown in excess.

And so he denied it. Because he knew that was the long, dark path to hell, and though he'd started his life on that path, he'd done his damnedest to find a new place to walk.

But for the moment, he was out of restraint. Because of Leah.

She parted her lips and kissed him deeply, his tongue sliding against hers. And because it seemed right, because he wanted to, he nipped her lush bottom lip, soothed away the pain.

The little sound that escaped her wasn't one of pain but of pleasure, and the encouragement spurred him on. He was consumed with this new craving, to have his fill of her taste, sweeter than candy, twice as tempting.

Dark and sweet.

Holding her tightly, he reversed their positions, put her back against the wall, both of his hands now deep in her hair, holding her to him. Her hands were everywhere. His shoulders, his back, down farther. She pulled him in tightly, his growing erection pressing against her stomach.

He was no detached observer to this kiss. He was drowning in it. Overtaken by it.

Shaking with it.

"Ajax," she whispered his name, her breath on his cheek.

Leah. He had Leah pressed up against a wall. Leah who had only agreed to marry him to save her business.

Leah, who made his defenses weak.

Leah, his wife. And yes, he would have an intimate relationship with her. At some point. But when he did, it would be on his terms. Not with him shaking like an addict denied his fix.

He pulled away from her, looked at her lips, swollen, red, not from the lipstick anymore, but from his kiss. He wanted to trace her lush lips with his thumb, follow the line with his tongue. Kiss her again.

Instead he dropped his hands to his sides, curled them into fists to disguise the tremor in them.

"That is enough for tonight, I think." He backed away from her, headed to the stairs.

"You think so?" she asked. "Because I think it was only the start."

He should give in. He should pull her into his arms, carry

her up the stairs, take her to his room and throw her on the bed. Give them both what their bodies wanted now.

Because it shouldn't matter to him. He shouldn't feel edgy and beyond himself. Shouldn't feel like he was about to lose himself, his control, utterly and completely.

He had been prepared to sleep with Rachel, after all, and the idea hadn't made him feel like he was losing his mind.

He tried to conjure a picture of the woman he loved. And he found it was hard. Tried to pick a fantasy he'd had of her, and realized there wasn't one. There had never been fantasies of Rachel, not like that. He'd known they would sleep together, and that had been enough. Because it would happen in the right time, according to the plan.

Because then…then everything would be complete. It would be right. But there had been no fantasies.

Even when working his body to the point of exhaustion before bed didn't keep sleeplessness or arousal at bay; when he took himself in hand, he never imagined a specific woman. No, he did his best to banish images, for fear that he would call up the wrong ones. Images of a past stained beyond the point of ever washing clean.

In those moments he imagined softness, heat, a breathy sound of desire in his ear. Like Leah had made tonight.

No. He wouldn't do this. He wasn't a slave to his body.

Then why the hell can't you stop shaking?

"I'll let you know when I'm ready to start with you, Leah," he bit out. "And when I do, you had better be certain, because when it happens, there will be no stopping."

If he let it go, if this feeling roaring inside of him ever slipped its leash, he knew there would be no way he could stop.

Flashes of memory went through his mind. Women's hands on his body. Practiced kisses. And then a girl, crying in the corner of the bed as though a monster were after her.

He had to stop now. He had to get his control back.

If he didn't, he would become a slave to it.

CHAPTER SIX

AJAX DIRECTED EVERY curse he knew, and there were many, at the media the next morning. Were it not for the media, he could escape his new bride for a little while, since pressing business demanded his presence at Holt Headquarters in New York.

But the media prevented it.

Though, in truth, it was not just the media. Leah would be badly missed by everyone on staff, from the woman at front desk reception to the man who cleaned the wastebaskets at night, if he showed up, newly married to the beloved heiress, without her in tow.

Yes, he was well and truly stuck.

He needed distance, a chance to regain a firm grip on himself, and he wasn't getting it.

He stormed into the study to find Leah, legs curled up beneath her, her laptop in front of her, a piece of red licorice dangling from her lips.

The combination of items brought him straight back to last night. Candy. Red. Lips.

The kiss.

He ran through another string of multilingual curses in his mind.

"We have to go to New York," he said, his words harsher than intended.

She arched her brows and sucked the piece of candy into her mouth, chewing thoughtfully before speaking. "Do we?"

"Yes. It seems your quality control issues weren't the only ones. Nothing like starting the takeover of a business with serious problems. So, I have to go and figure out where the weak link in the chain is, personally, or there will be no more Holt to worry about."

"You're being dramatic."

"A little," he said. "But I do not want to lose ground within my first week of ownership, and preferably not ever. Wouldn't Christofides love that?"

"I'm sure."

"That means I need to be there now. And you need to come with me."

"I suppose it would look wrong if I didn't go."

"Almost as bad as not showing up for a wedding. It would start to appear I couldn't do anything but repel women."

She laughed. "I doubt anyone would think you *repel* women. Although, sometimes you do have bad manners."

"Bad manners?"

"And you're a little hard to deal with."

"Am I?"

"If you don't know that, then you're out of touch with reality."

"I like things the way I like them. I like them to go according to plan."

She stood and stretched, rounded breasts pushed against the fabric of her T-shirt. And he couldn't stop his eyes from going there. Couldn't stop the memory of what it had felt like to have them pressed against his chest.

So soft. So feminine. So utterly different from him.

"And when things don't go according to plan you get completely surly."

"I cannot deny it. But then, in my defense, in my adult years very little has gone against my plan, and I'm out of practice in dealing with improvising."

"Nothing would dare go against you normally…you're far too scary."

"Scary?" He found the descriptor odd. More than that, he didn't like it. It made him remember things that were best left buried.

He didn't go out of his way to be scary. Neither was he particularly fun, and he knew that. But the things in life that so many people seemed to find fun had a dark underbelly that he'd spent his early years trapped beneath.

If a rich guy wanted to go and get high at a party, the drug had to come from somewhere. If someone wanted to pay for a little sex, or watch a graphic video, those women, those men had to come from somewhere.

He had seen those people. Their pain. Worse, he had been a part of it. He had caused it.

A mansion had to be paid for. The money had to come from somewhere.

As a boy he hadn't known that. He'd wandered around that mansion, unsupervised, and had taken all that was on offer. Whatever food was in the kitchen. Whatever substance was left unlocked.

And later, whatever woman was available.

But then he had learned that for every bit of fun there was a price. All that glittered was dark and tarnished beneath.

He knew.

Other people might be able to stick their head in the sand and pretend it wasn't true. They might be able to indulge themselves in the meaningless things in life, spending money, worthless paper, on what had cost others their souls.

But he couldn't do it. And yes, that made him a bit un-fun. But the alternative was depravity. And he had run from that. Had run away at sixteen, had changed his name, had changed islands.

"You're a bit severe," she said.

"I'm practical, which I realize is difficult to take for some people. People who lead with emotions rather than with logic."

"Logic doesn't explain everything. It doesn't have all the answers," she said, bending down and picking up another piece of licorice from the coffee table, lifting it to her lips. "Candy isn't logical. It's not very good for you. It can rot your teeth. But we like it." She took a bite and smiled.

If anyone made him want to forget the rot and taste the sweet, it was her.

The realization jolted him.

"Because people are stupid," he bit out. "And again that's feeling and not logic. You like candy so even though it's bad for you and contributes nothing to your life, you eat it."

"I don't just eat it, I sell it. I create it."

"So, your entire life's work is based around something wholly unnecessary."

"But something people like, Ajax. I make people happy."

"And give them cavities."

She laughed. He'd always liked the sound of her laugh. It wasn't genteel or restrained. It was just…feeling. Funny how, though he stripped down his feelings to the bare essentials, he'd always enjoyed watching hers.

Because she'd never had them stolen. Because she didn't know about all the horrors in life.

A woman like Leah didn't need to know.

A strange surge of protectiveness ran through him. The urge to protect her from that darkness, and from anything that had touched it was so strong he nearly doubled over with it. The urge to protect her from himself.

But that was an impossibility. She was his wife. He was her husband. He would touch her with his hands, and it would spread to her.…

And they had to go to New York.

"Scary or not," he said, "you are coming to the States with me."

She shrugged. "Great. It is great, actually. Most of my things are there and all. And I need to pay a visit to the shop there. I like to frequent the stores. Especially the big ones."

"A working trip for both of us."

She nodded slowly, her eyes rising to meet his, as if she was trying to read his thoughts.

"What?" he asked.

"What what?"

"You are concentrating so hard I can hear you thinking."

"I'm thinking about last night." She took another bite of licorice.

"What about it?"

"That scintillating conversation with those two businessmen. Except no, not that. Our kiss."

The thought of it sent a rash of heat across his skin. He would have to stop and examine that later. How that could happen when the temperature in the room was constant. How he could feel that without giving himself permission?

The simple answer was that it was Leah's fault. She was doing things to him. And he had no idea how she held that power. How, when he had thought himself in love with another woman. When he'd held on to his control for so long.

"What about it?"

"I'm wondering why we're bothering to defer anything. I think it was pretty clear last night what we both wanted."

"And we'll have it, but when we have time to focus on that." Again, he felt edgy, restless. Not ready to confront the physical part of their relationship.

It was because of her, he decided. Because it had been rushed. Because what she'd done, for the company, and for him, was very much like selling herself. And he felt uneasy about it. If he had a doubt that she wanted him, wanted to be in the marriage, it would make him feel like he was one of his father's henchman after all. And that was why he'd run away in the first place. To escape that fate, no matter what.

You. In my bed. Every night.

She'd said it, but the vows were spoken. And whether or not she would ever admit it, she was bound to him. And that put her in his care. And if he didn't care for her, then it put her under his thumb, and he would be damned if he was ever that man.

"When?"

"On our honeymoon. I did have one planned. It's in two weeks. That should give ample time to get everything sorted out at Holt, for you to deal with any issues your stores are having due to the quality control glitch, and for us to have convinced the press that everything is, in fact, fine in our relationship."

It would give him time, so that he didn't feel like a marauder, mindlessly claiming husbandly rights simply because she was his bride. And whether or not she cared if he thought of another woman while they were in bed together, he found he did.

He didn't have the stomach for using people. And that was, in his mind, what it would be.

He'd had his fill of using people. He couldn't use Leah, too. Not like that. He could not make her a prostitute, paying her in the form of safety for her company.

And he couldn't make love to her while he had feelings for someone else.

Although, it was becoming harder to picture Rachel. With the memory of his and Leah's kiss burned into his mind, a watermark over his every thought for the past twelve hours, it was hard to think at all.

And that made it harder to pretend it was the reason he hadn't touched his wife. He pushed the thought aside. Of course it was a reason. It was practically *the* reason.

"Two weeks? And then we just start…living as a real married couple."

"It has to happen sometime. Preferably when we can focus on each other."

"I see…and…and besides sex, what is marriage to you,

Ajax? Is it love? Is it companionship? Friendship? What will I be to you?"

"I...I will share your bed," he said, his voice rough. "I will protect you. I will give you children. If you reach out in the dark...I will be there."

These were his real marriage vows. His promises to her. And he found he meant them. That he would carve them onto the remains of his soul if necessary.

He was changing direction, but this was still a path he could walk. Love wasn't necessary. There was no need for a heavy, emotional attachment. Not when there was honesty. Not when there was faithfulness. Loyalty.

He wasn't even certain now if he knew what love was. Rachel had been the symbol of his dreams. His finish line in so many ways. She had come to mean so much to him in what she had represented that it had been easy to imagine it was love.

But now he wondered. Leah had accused him of seeing Rachel as an ideal, not as a woman. Perhaps that was true.

Perhaps he was simply incapable of love. In a strange way, he found that comforting. Love was an awfully big emotion, one he imagined was hard to control. He couldn't have such a thing.

"Nothing more?" she asked.

"That is everything, Leah. From me, that is everything."

She looked away from him, lifted her hand and scrunched her ponytail, the curls springing back the moment she released it. And he remembered sifting his fingers through it last night. It had been straighter then. He wondered how it felt with all the curl in it. She bit her lower lip, and he remembered doing the same last night. And the little sound of pleasure she'd made.

His stomach tightened, and so did his groin. His lack of control stunned him enough that it took a while to get any back. All he could do was look at her, look at her and focus on the heat that was coursing through his body.

"I am giving you everything," he said slowly, "because

you're my wife. And there is no other woman who holds that position now or ever. No matter how the marriage started."

"Thanks, Ajax," she said, her voice a whisper, sadness in her eyes.

He wanted to offer her more. To offer her comfort. The problem was, he was the last person on earth who should ever be allowed to offer comfort. To give tenderness.

Because if he ever let the walls down, the darkness would start to bleed out.

Normally going back to Holt felt like coming home. But Leah didn't feel at home when she walked through the glass revolving doors and into the familiar, gray-marble lobby.

It was the same, but everything had changed. Her father wasn't here. He was in Rhodes. And while there was nothing too unusual about that—ever since her father had first visited the island, he'd been in love with it and had made it a second home—there was no longer a desk here with his name on it, and that did make it different.

Holt Enterprises had always been Joseph Holt's domain. Now it belonged to Ajax. And it belonged to her. Interesting because she'd never imagined that happening. Now that it had…now that it had she realized how much she valued being a part of it.

Because Holt was important. To her, to her future children, to the people who worked here. And to Ajax. Ajax loved Holt. She couldn't fault him there. He would do the very best he could by it, and if the success of Ajax's personal corporation was any indicator, the best he could do was very good indeed.

His husband skills were a bit more murky.

But the vow he'd made to her in the study at his home, where he had made plain the importance he put on her position as his wife…that gave her hope at least. Hope that things could be good. Better than they were. And it made her want to lower her defenses a little bit.

It made her want to try.

As they walked through the reception area, almost empty at this hour of the night, most of staff gone home, she had a strange sense of déjà vu. How often had she followed him like this back when she'd been a teenager? Before she'd put up her walls. Before she'd been aware of how she looked to other people.

Trailing behind him, gabbing about something or another, soaking in every ounce of attention he gave her. Trying to get him to look at her. Trying to make him smile.

At the time, she'd felt like he was her friend. Like he might have feelings for her. As an adult, she saw herself for what she was: a delusional, chubby girl, following around an older, sophisticated man who had no time to listen to her drone on about her plans for her future candy shop.

And yet he had. He had never once been unkind or made her feel unwanted. If he had, she probably wouldn't have retained her crush for so long.

Even now she wasn't immune to him.

That kiss...

She followed him into an elevator and crossed her arms beneath her breasts while he pushed all the appropriate buttons. She'd had fantasies about him and elevators. All the times they'd ridden up in them together. In her very fevered teenage imagination she'd pictured him pulling her into his arms and bending her backward, kissing her neck, her lips.

All very impassioned at the time, but her imagination could do better than that now.

Yes, the fantasies she could spin about an elevator now were not half so innocent. They picked up where they'd left off the night before. With her against the wall. And her skirt shoved up around her hips—never mind that she was wearing dress pants at the moment—and him putting his hands between her thighs to help answer the pounding ache that was threatening to...

"So," she said, overly bright, trying to blot out the images running rampant through her mind, "do you have any artwork picked out for your office yet?"

He gave her a strange look. "No."

"Well, you'll want to…personalize it, right?"

"No. I won't be working from here. Someone else will be put in charge."

"You'll have an office, though."

"Yes, but I won't be spending much time in it."

"Your lack of desire for frivolous things is sort of annoying, Ajax. Do you have any idea how obnoxious it is to try and make small talk with someone when they don't seem to think about anything small?"

"I'm sorry I can't accommodate your need for me to care about trivial things."

"You suck at conversation—do you know that?"

"It's not this hard with everyone."

"It didn't used to be this hard with me. What changed?"

He arched a brow. "You stopped talking to me."

Oh. Right. So she had.

"I suppose I did." She followed him down the hall, and she was assaulted by another punch of the familiar. How many times had they walked like this? And how had she missed that even though she was walking with him, she was walking alone.

He didn't need her there. He didn't want her there. He just… accepted her presence. It seemed like there had to be more. Like they needed to find more. But she was trapped between her desire to protect herself, and her need to make more from her marriage than just two people who could barely make eye contact.

That was why the candy she'd bought him was in her purse, and not already sitting on his desk. Because she hadn't decided what she was going to do with it yet.

He pushed open the door to what had been her father's office. The pictures on the wall were gone. His nameplate on his desk, gone. She swallowed, or at least she tried to. A lump stopped her accomplishing it.

"Wow. I guess it really is yours now."

"He was prompt in removing his things," Ajax said, looking around the space.

"Ajax…" She bit the inside of her cheek, trying to stop the question, the random, stupid, insistent question that wanted to come out at this, of all times, but she couldn't stop it. "Did you sleep with my sister?"

His focus zeroed in on her, his expression one of shock. Well, shock for Ajax, which meant a raised brow and deeper frown than normal. "Why would you ask that?"

"Morbid, oh Lord is it ever morbid, curiosity. I know you told me never to compare myself to her, but in this instance… well, I need to know if you'll be comparing us." She flinched, because really, what were the odds that Ajax had never slept with Rachel? They'd been together for a long time, and Ajax was an incredibly sexy, virile man. Leah never, ever, ever in a million years would have been able to keep her hands off him for all that time.

Hell, she'd attacked him and pushed him against a wall after two days of close proximity.

"I told you that?" he asked, turning back to the desk, then back to her, as if he wasn't sure where he was supposed to be looking.

"Not to compare myself? Yes. Don't you…do you remember that?" She looked at his expression, his eyes blank. He didn't remember. How stupid to think that he would. That one of the defining moments in her life, in deciding how to act in public, how to deal with the press, would even register on his radar. So very, very telling.

"Anyway… I just… I wanted to know," she finished, her words hollow in the silence.

"We didn't."

"What?" The admission pushed the air from her lungs. "How is that even possible?"

"We were going to wait until we married," he said, the words tugged from him, the topic clearly one he wasn't interested in addressing.

"I...I didn't expect that."

"Why not?"

"Most men would pressure a girl to get sex as quickly as possible. Why should I believe you're any different?"

"I am," he said, his tone light, a dark glint in his eyes that told her his voice was fraudulent. "I am not like most men." He moved toward her, his expression unchanging. Her heart stopped, her stomach folding in on itself. His eyes never wavered from hers, and she wondered, she hoped, that he would touch her. Kiss her. He dipped his head, traced her jaw with the tip of his finger. "I am much, much worse."

He pulled away from her and her breath left her body in a rush. She blinked, feeling dizzy, feeling like she was coming out of some sort of trance.

He wasn't going to answer her. She felt like there was a wall between them. Made of ice and his feelings for another woman. And she wanted to scream at him. For not being the man she'd wanted him to be. The man she'd thought he was.

And that wasn't really fair, was it? To be angry at him for not being like she imagined. And it really didn't make sense that it should hurt so much.

She reached into her purse, her fingers curling around the little box of truffles she'd put in there. Her olive branch. Her attempt to make things work better between them.

But not now.

She knew better than this. Knew that you had to protect yourself, or all of your insides would get pulled out and put on display for the public. Ridiculed. She wasn't dropping her shields for him.

She wasn't going to expose herself to that kind of pain. The idea of letting him in, of putting herself out there and trying to make their marriage more than just a plan, had obviously been a stupid one.

She released her hold on the box and turned away from him. "I'm going to go back to my penthouse and try to make arrangements for my things."

"Good. Be back at my house tonight."

"Why?"

"Appearance, *agape,* why else?"

"Oh, no. Yeah. Of course." She wanted to say something tart. To lash out at him. Certainly not so he could be with her. Or something like that. But her throat was too raw and her head hurt. And she wouldn't risk revealing that to him. "See you later then. I'll try to make some sort of big hand gesture and maybe do a pantomime of being trapped in a box so I get the paparazzi's attention as I go back to the house. Wouldn't want them to miss me being there. For appearances."

"Whatever you feel you need to do."

Yell at you until I forget how confused I am. "Great. See you later."

Ajax watched Leah leave, a strange weight settling in his stomach. She'd looked…upset, and that was an understatement. But he hadn't wanted to have a conversation with her about sex, not when his body still burned from their kiss.

And he hadn't wanted to admit that he'd never slept with Rachel. Pride? He'd never thought he would suffer from male pride in quite that way. He'd made his choices. Very deliberately and he was hardly going to regret them now.

He looked down at his desk. It looked empty. Because Joseph Holt wasn't here. He'd removed his presence, and Ajax found that he missed the presence of his mentor.

If there was ever a man he wanted to imitate, it was him.

Unlike his own father, Joseph Holt was a good man. He cared for his family, for people, his staff. He worked hard and found a reward in it. There was an honesty to him, a humanity that had been completely foreign to Ajax when he'd first shown up at the estate, a lost boy with scars inside that would never heal properly.

And Joseph Holt had taken him in and shown him there was another way to live, another way to act than the way he'd seen all of his life. Than the dirty, disgusting hell he'd been brought up in. A hell he'd nearly jumped into with both feet.

He sat down at the desk. *His* desk now. And he only hoped that with the absence of Joseph, and all of his things, he would still be able to be the man he'd taught him to be.

And then it suddenly hit him why his desk looked so empty. A strange memory from the past that seemed prominent now.

Leah hadn't left him any candy.

CHAPTER SEVEN

THE DAYS IN New York were basically miserable. Leah avoided Ajax to the best of her ability. She spent time at her shop and her lab, experimenting with flavors.

She didn't do a lot of hands-on candy creation, not at this stage in her career, but when she was feeling stressed it was a nice distraction.

But her two weeks was coming to an end. In just a few minutes. And that meant it was nearly honeymoon time. Romance time.

With a man she was barely speaking to. Yay. That was just freaking spiffy.

She was meeting him at the airport, because they'd both been too busy to get a car together. Well, no, that was a lie. She could have made time, but she'd lied and said she didn't have it so she could avoid him for a few extra moments.

Now she was sitting there in the private lounge, waiting for him to come, with bags of candy wrapped in ribbon scattered around her feet. She always took the surplus stock, and this time she'd ended up with a bunch of irregular chocolate shoes thanks to the factory snafu.

It would be really nice if the honeymoon was severely depressing. Binge eating easily accessed. She honestly had no idea what to expect from Ajax, so she'd come prepared.

The door to the lounge opened, and Ajax walked in, looking unbelievably sexy in a black suit with a black tie. The man was buttoned up and knotted to perfection, short hair in place. Everything about him shouted control freak. And she had no idea what it was in her that found it so attractive. She just wanted to loosen that tie, undo his buttons and run her fingers through his hair and get it all messy.

She sucked in a sharp breath and bent down, trying to gather up her candy. "Hi," she said, scooping the cellophane bags up, the packaging crinkling as she pulled them in tight to her chest. "I'm just… I got all this candy and I have to, get it now.…" She picked up a few more bags and nearly lost one. He took a step toward her at the same time she took one toward him. "Here." She dumped the bags into his arms. "Take. Please." Then she bent down and grabbed the rest, and her purse. "Ready?"

He arched a brow at her. "Everything is ready. Your bags are on board."

"Great. Thanks. So…where are we going?"

"Did I not mention?"

"No, it's one of those silly little incidentals we've never talked about. Like what your favorite color is, the real nature of your relationship with my sister…that kind of thing."

"Are you really bringing that up again now?" he asked, holding the door open for her. She walked out in front of him and started through the terminal, headed to the exit where the private planes were parked, ready for takeoff.

"I guess so. I hadn't planned to. But I hadn't really planned to the first time. I'm suffering from a case of terminal honesty at the moment."

"It's not as charming as one might think."

"Oh, I don't think it's charming. I think it's hideously embarrassing. I aim to stop it as soon as possible."

"Anytime you see fit."

She led the way out onto the tarmac. "Which plane is yours?"

"The big one," he said, without a trace of humor. All she could hear was the potential double entendre.

She arched a brow. "Indeed." She walked up the stairs that led to the interior of the jet. They'd flown in it on the way to New York, but still, to her, a plane on the runway looked like a plane on the runway.

The inside, however, was what truly distinguished it from anything she'd ever seen before. Plush carpets, leather furniture, a flat-screen television and a bedroom made it more comfortable than most Manhattan apartments. And twice as big as some of them, too.

She'd been raised wealthy, and she was used to opulence. To a degree. Ajax's version was on a whole other level. It wasn't showy, not in an obvious way. No gold-plated toilet paper roll holders.

It was in the quality of the leather on the couch, the type of wine being served. The glass the wine was in.

Ajax set her bags down on the couch and took a seat next to them. So she opted for the chair across the room from him. Safer.

"Now, tell me where we're going," she said.

"You don't want to be surprised?"

"The wedding was my surprise," she said dryly. "Let me in on the honeymoon destination."

"St. Lucia."

"Oh, wow." For some reason, the image of the beautiful island, one she'd never been to, but had seen pictures of, made her throat close up. Maybe because she knew he'd planned to take Rachel there. And it was easy to see Rachel happy in a place like that. Lounging on the beach, smiling at her new husband. Holding his hand while they walked through the surf.

He'd planned that for her.

Why did the thought sneak up on her like that sometimes? Why did she care? Why did she care about him or the honeymoon or anything? It would be so much easier if she could just be like him. With a big fat vacancy sign hanging on her chest.

She could be married to him, run her business, go to events

with him and get him naked at the end of the night and never care who he was thinking of or what he felt.

But that wasn't her. It wasn't how she was. She'd had to get tough when she'd made her leap into the world of business, had had to change the way she behaved in public and in private, really.

But with Ajax…sometimes he made her feel like the girl she'd been. He made her feel soft. Exposed. She didn't like it. Especially not when she'd just purposed to double down her efforts protecting herself.

She felt like she had a knot of confusion living in her stomach. Which made eating difficult. Well, eating anything but candy.

Good thing she'd brought a bunch with her.

Ajax pulled his laptop out of his briefcase and turned his focus to the screen. The conversation was clearly over.

Well, that was fine. She could just sit there and eat candy. And think about their honeymoon, which, now that she knew where they were going, she knew was sure to be filled with sun and sand.

And for now, she wouldn't think of anything else.

The rich blues and greens of St. Lucia felt even more vibrant and saturated after spending two weeks in the gray of New York City. Leah had always liked the city, but the ocean had always felt more like home to her.

This felt more like home.

Ajax had rented them a private villa for the duration of their stay, a massive structure made of rough-hewn wood, with a wide stretch of white sand to the front of it, backed by mountains and dense trees.

It was straight out of a fantasy. Too bad she was no longer under the delusion that her husband was, too.

"How long were you planning on this being your honeymoon destination?" she asked. Why had she asked? She didn't really want to know. Curse her stupid curiosity.

"More than a year. When we set the wedding date, I booked this place."

"You do like your plans, don't you?"

"Without a plan, how do you know if you're on the right path?"

"I don't know. If you adhere so tightly to a plan, how do you know you're not missing something really great that's just a hair to your left?"

He shrugged and walked up the steps that led into the villa. "It isn't worth the risk," he said. "Not to me."

He pushed the door open and went inside; Leah followed, scanning the surroundings. It was a giant, open room with a vaulted ceiling, accented by exposed beams. The floor was made from wood, too, rough and unfinished, giving the impression of something rustic in the midst of the polished luxury. The bedroom was only partitioned off from the main living area by a swathe of gauzy fabric. And beyond the veil, a large, plush bed that was certainly built for two.

And they weren't going to need separate sleeping quarters. She looked ahead, at Ajax's broad back, his trim hips and... well, yeah the way his black dress pants fit over his muscular butt. That was a perk to walking behind Ajax chatting his ear off she'd discovered a little later into her teens. The view from back there was good.

"What risk? The risk of failure?" she asked.

"No. Failure would not be half so bad. There are much bigger things, much darker things to fear." He set down the bag he'd been carrying and walked toward the far end of the room. "Let me ask you a question, Leah."

"Go for it."

"Do you think you're a good person?"

She blinked. "Yes. I...suppose so. I make candy, not war,

and I smile at people when I walk by them on the street. Never took money from my grandma's purse. Yes."

"All right, but do you trust that if your circumstances changed, you would remain a good person? That you would have morals, morals that took hold deep inside of you, that would keep you from ever changing?"

"I'd like to think so," she said, sensing she wouldn't like where he was leading her.

"I trust that I am not a good person. Not just that I might not be if things were to change, but that if I ever take my eyes off the prize in front of me, if I let myself slip up, I will go right back into the darkness I came out of, and I'm not willing to do it. Not just for me. For everyone I might hurt. Emotion, need, lust—those things distract. They are unpredictable. I don't trust them."

She laughed a little, not because anything he said was funny but because it was the only way she could release the tension, the unease, building inside of her.

"You wouldn't…hurt anyone, Ajax."

He laughed, and his was obviously not born of humor, either. "Oh, you say that, Leah, but you don't know anything about me, not really. You think you do. You think I was born the minute I appeared on your family's estate? No. By then… by then I had lived more life in sixteen years than a girl like you will have lived at the end of her days. And that's not an insult. You don't want to have seen what I've seen. To know what I've done. I don't want to know it. But I do. And the memory is what keeps me going this way. It's what reminds me, every day, of how important it is to keep your eyes on the goal."

"Ajax…"

"We're done talking about this."

"No, we aren't," she said. "You told me yesterday that you were worse than most men. Today you're telling me you've done things… I think I deserve to have an idea of what I'm dealing with here."

"Why? I thought you knew me so well?"

"No. I knew your mask. And I liked it better."

"Everyone does," he said. "And they should. On that note—" he reached for his tie, loosened it and then pulled it off "—I think I'll go for a swim." Then he started undoing the buttons on his shirt, stripping so he was bare to the waist. Oh...my.

It was so easy to forget how angry she was, how hurt and confused when she saw that lean, well-defined torso. All olive skin with a bit of dark hair over his chest. Broadcasting just how masculine he was. As if she needed the reminder.

He headed toward the bedroom area, and she just stopped, staring. He was behind the curtain, but she could see, easily, the silhouette of him through the thin gauze. He opened one of the bags that had been delivered ahead of them and pulled out swim shorts, then he pushed his pants and underwear down his thighs.

And as he stripped the clothes away from his skin, the armor was ripped from her body.

She should look away. He wasn't putting on a show for her. She had no right or reason to stand there staring at all that skin, hard, well-defined thighs, the butt...and...and...her brain stopped working when she caught a small glimpse of the front of him, still heavily obscured by the fabric. But the dark shadow there at the apex of his thighs was enticing nonetheless.

He raised his gaze, his eyes clashing with her as he tugged his swim shorts up and over the place she was currently ogling, then he stepped out from the behind the curtain.

"See anything you like?" he asked.

She puckered her lips. "Lots, actually. But then, that's a good thing, right? All things considered?"

"Am I supposed to blush and stammer now?" he asked, his tone dry.

She'd seen Ajax in swim shorts plenty of times, but this was different. They were alone. There was a bed. And she'd just seen his very naked silhouette. "I wouldn't dream of that," she said. "After all, you've seen things I can't even imagine."

"Don't forget." He walked past her and out the door. And then she realized what he was doing. He was avoiding her. Avoiding the potential intimacy of the moment.

He was so not getting away with that.

She stalked back into the bedroom area and opened her suitcase, rummaging around until she found her swimsuit. It was a one-piece, black. Serviceable. It was not what she wanted. He wasn't allowed to be the only one who could inspire lust-fueled brain failure.

She ignored the voice that told her she probably wasn't capable of inspiring it. That voice could suck it.

She needed to make a quick trip to the resort shops.

A swim did a little to cool the burn in Ajax's blood. But the water wasn't as cold as he needed it to be. It wasn't arousal. At least, it wasn't only arousal that was firing through his system.

But the moment he'd walked into that room, looked at Leah and that bed, he'd realized that it was going to happen, and that he wanted it to. And with that had been a collision with reality. Leah had been manipulated into being here. This place had been chosen for another woman. And he had simply brought her here as if she and Rachel were interchangeable, and he knew full well they were not.

For a start, Rachel hadn't made him feel like his blood was going to boil over and reduce to nothing. Leah on the other hand was testing the bonds of his control. Was making him want things he hadn't craved in years.

He'd been so close to pushing her down onto that bed when they'd first walked in. To kissing her until she lost that sad look, until he made the room theirs and exorcised the ghost of the woman he'd intended to bring into it.

And then he'd had to remind himself why he must keep control. Why he had to remember what sort of man he was.

Of course, with Leah there would be no drugs involved. Of course not. He hadn't touched them in seventeen years. Not even tempted to. Not after the last time.

Still, he couldn't separate sex from the chaos and shame that lingered in the air at his father's home. Couldn't separate it from that last night there. From that haze, that feeling of being out of control. Of everything being skewed and confused. And one frightened woman. A woman he had frightened.

No, he didn't want to think about it. But he had to. He had to remember. So he would remember why control was so important.

"Oh, good, you're still here."

He turned around at the sound of Leah's voice and his throat went dry. The memory he'd been replaying was wiped out completely. Now all he could see was curves, soft, pale skin.

And a red bikini that should be illegal. It tied at her rounded hips, and it seemed, to him, that it would be the easiest thing to release those ties. The top was the same, barely covering her breasts. Her stomach wasn't cut or defined like many of the women he saw at the beaches at the exclusive resorts he frequented, compliments of exercise or a skilled surgeon. No, she was simply Leah. Simply a woman.

In that moment it was her softness, her roundness, that made her seem wholly, purely female. There was a natural quality to her shape, to her movements.

For a moment, just a moment, his view of sex, the things he'd seen, the things he'd done, were erased. And there was only Leah.

"Yes, I am. Where have you been?" he asked, willing his body under control before he took a step out of the water and started toward where she stood on the white sand beach.

"Shopping."

"For?"

"All kinds of things," she said. "Mainly this." She put her

hand on her hip, indicating the bikini, he imagined. Not that there was much of it to indicate.

"What else?"

She met his eyes. "Underwear. The kind you want someone to see."

Heat shot through him, starting in his stomach, pooling in his groin. "Really?" His voice sounded rough. Not like his own.

"Yes. You seem interested."

There was no lying about it. It would be too obvious. And anyway, why should he? She was his wife. She wanted him. He wouldn't be forcing himself on her.

She did want him. And not just because she had to be here with him. She'd made her choice. She had.

"I am." His voice was unsteady, a stranger's voice.

"I'm glad."

"Does that mean you're ready? Here? Now?" He wasn't. Not while he felt like this.

"No. It's nice to have a little buildup, don't you think? Nice to anticipate."

She had no idea how damn long he'd been anticipating.

"I don't know if *nice* is the word I'd use."

She took a step toward him, her steps unsteady as her feet sank into the deep sand, her breasts bouncing with the motion.

And he felt like he was a teenage boy. Not the teenage boy he'd been with unlimited access to sex. Sex that had been, at its heart, twisted, one-sided, a commodity. Sex in his world was used for the pleasures of the rich, powerful and debauched.

There was something dark to his encounters in the past, to lust as he knew it. It wasn't this jittery feeling in his veins, this shot of anticipation and pure excitement. This desire to give, not just to take. To caress, not just possess.

And also uncertainty. She made him feel off balance. A side effect of things not going according to his plan. Or maybe just a side effect of her beautiful figure.

She extended her hand, touched his face. "I don't know—

it's nicer than fighting, which is the only other thing we seem to be able to do. Fight and kiss."

And the reins holding him back snapped. He dipped his head and captured her lips, quick and hard, too desperate for a taste to wait. When he broke the kiss, her eyes were round, her mouth swollen.

"Oh," she said.

"What?" he asked, afraid for a second he'd overstepped his bounds. But he'd been sure this was what she was here for. Flirtation. Seduction.

He knew what it looked like when women wanted him. Women had always wanted him, especially since he'd started earning money. He turned them down, but it didn't mean he didn't recognize what it looked like when a woman had sex on her mind.

"Sorry, you just knocked all my thoughts out of my head."

"Is that…good?" he asked.

"Yeah. Just… I don't think I can think of anything witty to say for at least a minute, so maybe you could just look away from my shame and leave me and my mushy brain in peace?"

"Are you going to swim?"

"I think you're supposed to wait a half hour to swim after having your brain scrambled."

"Is that a scientific fact?"

"No idea."

He smiled. Not because he wanted her to see him smile, not because he was conscious of needing to project an emotion. He smiled because he couldn't help himself. "I think…I think I should take you to dinner tonight."

"Romance?"

"Yes."

"You don't have to do that."

"I know. But I want to."

"Coming from you, Ajax, that's romance all by itself."

CHAPTER EIGHT

IT TOOK LEAH only an hour after the encounter on the beach to decide that she wasn't letting Ajax take her to dinner. And she had reasons and her own plan. A plan she was going to ambush him with. She didn't necessarily want romance. What she wanted was to feel as if she had some control. To feel like she wasn't simply being led around.

If there was one thing she'd learned about Ajax since their marriage a couple of weeks ago, it was that he lived in his head. To look at him, you wouldn't think it.

Tall, broad, muscular, he looked like a man who dealt in the physical. Like the promise of sex and sweat. But he was controlled by his mind. And he liked it that way.

And she didn't want him calculating his way through their marriage consummation. It would give him too much control.

One thing she did know: as strong as her feelings for him had been when she was a teenager, she hadn't loved him. There was a certain freedom in that. The kind of freedom that made her feel that maybe she didn't have to guard herself as closely as she'd thought.

She'd never really known Ajax. She'd imagined who she'd thought he might be because of polite conversation they'd made. Because he'd smiled at her, accepted her gifts. But she knew better than that now. You couldn't love a man you didn't know.

Of course, not loving him didn't mean not wanting him.

She did. She was so attracted to him her teeth ached. Among other things.

And she didn't want his restraint. She wanted him just as vulnerable as she was. Just as raw. Now her being a virgin put her at a massive disadvantage but she was just not going to think about all the thin sexy beauties, possibly including her sister, who had graced his bed. No, she was not.

Anyway, he wanted her. She'd seen the look in his eyes.

She'd picked the bikini as a challenge, and as a test, for her own benefit. Because the last thing she'd wanted was for him to get her naked and for her to see shock and horror over her shape. She looked all right, but she didn't have that popular stick shape happening. She wasn't a runway model. She wasn't even a swimsuit catalog model, in spite of the boobs.

But he'd seen, and he wanted.

There was victory in that.

Now she planned on taking his control while his defenses were down.

Her evil plan to seduce the Greek billionaire was in full swing. And when she did…when she did maybe she could exorcise the feelings inside of her. Maybe it would give her some power. Or maybe it would just dull the intensity of feeling she had around him.

Even without the feelings, she was the backup bride. The second choice. The less-beautiful, less-written-about, less-celebrated Holt heiress.

She loved her sister. She truly did. And having to share media adoration, or rather split it 70/30 was fine. But to let Rachel have her husband's heart? That just felt unfair. She didn't love him. He didn't love her. But she did not want him to love someone else. Seemed reasonable to her.

But tonight, tonight wasn't about crushes. Or love. Or being second best. Tonight he was going to want *her*. And that was just about control. And sex.

As soon as he came back from the very urgent business he was taking care of down in the resort's main building.

She reached into the neckline of her dress and leaned forward, giving her breasts a quick boost. Hey, she knew her greatest assets, and she wasn't above trying to display them to their best effect. Basic seduction technique. She was pretty sure. She'd never seduced anyone before.

But then, she'd never been in a loveless, or any other kind of marriage, either. So all new territory.

She looked in the mirror and let out a slow breath. Yeah, she looked…almost not like herself. Lots of eye makeup, her breasts putting on a great show over the neckline of her dress, a dress that was super skintight. She was just going to go with the bombshell look. And yeah, when she turned sideways, her stomach didn't look totally flat, but oh well.

She was her. And she was going to seduce the man with what she had. Because she wasn't like the other women he probably preferred. But not even a good pair of control-top panty hose would make it so.

And when she was naked they wouldn't have helped anyway. No point in false advertising, not when he was going to be seeing the woman behind the curtain, so to speak.

Anyway, the bikini had showed him what he was getting. And the look in his eyes…it was burned into her mind. It was what was giving her confidence now.

The front door to the villa opened, and she turned. She could see him in the doorway, his silhouette clear through the curtain that partitioned off the living area.

"You're back," she said.

"Yes." She couldn't see his face in detail, and his voice was monotone. His expression was, in all likelihood, monotone, too, and probably wouldn't give her any more clues than his voice. "Are you ready to go out?"

She swept the curtain aside. "Not really."

"You look ready."

She put her hands on her hips, on the dress that was practically shrink-wrapped to her curves. "This isn't the kind of thing I normally wear out."

"Why not?" He looked her over, appraising, and a rush of heat went through her body.

"Because…well, it's just not."

"Are you going to change?"

"Are you going to play obtuse?"

He nodded slowly. "Perhaps."

"Don't." She crossed to him, until she was standing close enough to him that she could feel the heat radiating from his body. "It doesn't suit you. You're not the kind of man who can pull it off. You're far too experienced."

"Experienced? I don't know if that's the word I would use," he said, his expression like granite. "Jaded? Maybe."

"Either way, playing dumb isn't your game."

"Perhaps not, but you do make it hard to think."

"Do I?"

Ajax stood, his hands at his sides, fighting the urge to pull Leah into his arms, to strip off the chains that held him, once and for all. To say to hell with control and simply take what he wanted, what he was starving for.

Somehow, in all of this, Leah had started to become an obsession. A desire he couldn't shake or ignore. Somehow, the feelings he'd had for Rachel on what would have been their wedding day had been consumed by the flame of need he felt for Leah.

Sweet Leah. Who had grown into a sharp-tongued temptress with curves that called to fantasies pushed into the darkest corners of his soul. Fantasies that had never been given the chance to play in his mind, not completely. They'd hovered around the edges of consciousness, a mist that he'd kept from creeping in. But now he was overtaken by it.

It was easier to simply let it flood in now, block the path. Block the view of everything behind and everything ahead.

He'd never felt like this. Had never been a slave to his desires in the way he was now. He'd experienced sexual arousal—of course he had. But the truth was, he hadn't had sex in seventeen years. And desire, adult desire, a man to a woman, was utterly foreign to him. He'd ensured that it was.

Because he'd always believed, since he'd been awakened to the reality of who he was, what he was capable of becoming, that he had to wait until he could be sure he would have control. That it was in the right context.

That the woman was not simply there, allowing herself to be used in exchange for something. That the woman wanted it.

But in this moment nothing mattered. Because there was something about Leah that made the past feel not just foggy, but nonexistent.

He wanted to drown in that feeling. Be baptized in it. Come out clean and new.

An illusion, he knew it, but he wanted to cling to it. Just for a while.

She reached up and traced his cheek with her fingertip, her whiskey eyes on his. Tempting him in a way alcohol never had.

He wanted it. Wanted to taste what he'd denied himself for so long. To let the memories of the women in his father's mansion burn so that there was only this. Sweet, heady and clean. He wanted everything, and suddenly he felt like he couldn't get it fast enough.

Seventeen years of self-denial, and on his worst night, with need, repressed and hot coursing through him, he had never felt this close to the edge. Had never felt anything this urgent. But now he was shaking, felt like he needed her more than air. He tried to look at her and see the girl she'd been, tried to look and remember why there was a time he hadn't wanted her. Now he wasn't certain if there had been a time.

How could he have ever not seen this? How could he have ever not wanted?

A whisper of something, desire, fear, washed over his skin.

And a memory. A memory of a girl who always left him gifts. Who told him everything that was happening in her life. A girl who had made his heart, a heart he'd put on ice years ago, feel warm in a way no one else had.

Not even the woman he'd thought he'd loved.

He touched her face, softly, then traced her lower lip with his thumb. He had never touched a woman like this before. With reverence. With respect.

The memory of past encounters left him ashamed. Women in his old world, in his father's world, had been treated as objects. Some men had, too. But it was the women he'd had experience with. Women who had probably only said yes to him because he was the boss's son. Because they didn't want to find themselves thrown out of the mansion with no access to drugs. Or worse, sold off to another corner of the world with a "master" who would be less kind.

And his last encounter with a woman…it had been so rough. Horrifying in the end. The haze of drugs clouding him badly. He'd had more that night than he'd had before.

And why not? His father had given them to him. A birthday present. And it was so rare that his father ever paid any attention to him.

Why not enjoy his gifts? The fruits of their labor, his father had said. The evidence of just how good their product was. It wasn't the first time he'd sampled the drugs. He was human, a young man with endless access to excess, and he'd taken it. But not the variety or amount he'd had the night of his birthday.

And his father had encouraged him to sample their other product. Women. Yes, he'd dabbled with the prostitutes that were around the mansion before. But never the women his father had taken into human trafficking. He'd barely seen any of those women before.

You can break her in, boy. A virgin, I think. A gift for you. She might say no, but she doesn't mean it. I've paid her well to spread her legs. She'll give it up whether she wants to or not.

He pulled back from Leah and took a deep breath. He didn't want to think about that. Not now. Not ever. He'd atoned for that particular sin, or he'd at least done his best to make it right. He could still remember, though. Her face. Her fear. The tears. But as soon as he'd realized…as soon as he'd gotten a moment of clarity…

And then they'd both escaped. He'd seen her back to her family, mostly untouched. The only scars on her, the only man to try to do anything to her had been him. Her scars were created by his hand. But at least…at least he'd stopped.

Control had won in the end. And he had to see that it always did.

Leah was his wife. Leah had made vows. Leah wanted to be here. She hadn't been kidnapped. She hadn't been sold.

Wasn't she? For shares in her own company? For the ownership of Holt?

No. It wasn't the same.

It wasn't.

"Tell me you want me," he ground out, his voice rougher than intended. "Tell me."

Her eyes opened, her expression dazed. "I want you."

"With my name." He was desperate to hear it. Consent was essential. Not consent under duress. Not consent that was heavy with the weight of duty. He required desire.

She touched his face. "I want you, Ajax. What other man would I want?"

"Why did you marry me?"

"For Holt. For my business. And for you, because you worked too hard to lose it all."

"But you made the decision. You *wanted* to."

"No one forced me. You were there. My father was there. He would never have made me do it. No one even hinted about me marrying you. I did. It was my idea." She put her finger on his lip, traced it as he'd done to her. "And if you'll recall, I demanded intimacy as a part of my terms and conditions."

"I do. But why?"

"Women have hormones, too, Ajax, and I don't want to go satisfying things with someone who isn't my husband. If this marriage is real, we honor our vows."

"Something we agree on."

"You'll be faithful to me, too?"

"Of course."

"No matter what?"

"Who would I break my vows with?"

She let out a shuddering breath. "All my life, Ajax, I have felt like I was just behind her. Everyone who's compared us has found me lacking next to her. And you preferred her, too. You said you loved her."

He was going to say something about emotion. About how he wasn't sure he'd ever had any. He'd directed everything he had at loving Rachel because marrying her had seemed like such a good idea. But he wasn't sure he'd truly loved her. Once she was taken away as a goal, his feelings had gone, too.

He was sure he *hadn't* loved her. He felt nothing when he thought of her now, not a twinge in his heart, not even a tug of lust. He felt more when he thought of that girl with the tear-streaked face from seventeen years earlier than he did when he thought of the woman he'd meant to marry just a few short weeks ago.

And he started to tell her that. But it wasn't what came out. "You are not sharing my body with any other woman."

Something in her expression turned feral, fierce. "Damn right I'm not. You're married to me."

"No, that's not what I meant." Why was he saying this now? It didn't matter. If he explained, he would have to give hints about his past. But it had been so long, and this was different. A few rushed, youthful couplings that had left him feeling dirty were nothing like this. "I have not been with a woman since I was fifteen."

Her mouth dropped open, her lips rounded into an *O*. "What?"

"So it's closer to eighteen years, in truth."

"That…that's an entire legal adult worth of time," she said, taking a step back. "I don't believe you. Your…your abs are like…begging to be licked, and you're telling me that no woman in the past…all that time, has ever taken them up on that?"

"They have offered. I've refused."

She gaped for a moment, short, half words coming out of her mouth, then cutting off partway. Then she finally spoke. "No offense, but why? You're a man. Men like sex. Men don't usually say no to sex."

"No, Leah, they often don't. And I find the atmosphere that surrounds irresponsible sexual behavior to be something I want no part of."

"Not all sex is irresponsible."

"No. It's not. But…I always thought that it was best in the context of a relationship. As I was never in the position to have them, I…abstained. I already told you that I wanted to wait until marriage to be with Rachel."

He wouldn't tell her the whole story now. Not now. Not while she still looked at him like this.

"And you *could* wait?"

"Yes. Easily. I prize my control over everything else, Leah. If I decide to do something, I do it. If I decide not to, I don't."

"You should win a control trophy or something," she said. "But then…I guess you've never felt very passionately about anyone."

"No." It was the truth and he realized it now. If Rachel had made him feel like this…like Leah did, if she'd made him shake…could he have held himself back?

"Because…because if you had, well…if she'd wanted you, I don't think you would have said no."

"Maybe that's true." A disquieting thought.

"But…but now?"

"We're married," he said. "This is…right."

"Right," she said, her amber eyes glistening. "Why did you tell me?"

He frowned. "Because it is honest."

"You're practically a virgin."

"I'm not," he said, his voice hard. "I am no innocent."

The conversation made him uncomfortable. Maybe that was male pride. Maybe he wasn't as different from other men now as he'd imagined. Not as immune to the stupid things men measured success by. He knew that there was nothing greater in following your base urges. Nothing more respectable. Any man could have all the sex he wanted. Control was the real strength, and he knew it. Yet, he still felt a measure of shame admitting his status to his wife.

"You don't look like one, that's for sure," she said, looking at him closely.

"Do I not?"

"You've seen too many things. It's reflected in your eyes." She reached out and traced the line of his brow before pulling away. "What have you seen, Ajax?"

He shook his head. "Things you have not. I won't burden you."

"But like you said…you weren't born the day you showed up at my father's estate."

"The man I am now is. And that man is the one who's going to make love with you tonight. Not the one I was. Not the one I might have become."

"But I want to know what made you who you are."

"No. Leah, you cannot want that. Please, the way you're looking at me now, the way you looked at me before, I will have that for tonight. Please."

She nodded slowly. "Okay. I'll take what you can give. For tonight."

"I do not know where to begin. I look at you…and there is so much I want."

A deep rose stained her cheeks, but her eyes never wavered from his. "Then we may have a problem, because I look at you and…I ache. And I really don't know where to start. Because I'm not just practically a virgin. I am one."

"Now that seems impossible to me."

"What?"

"How so many men didn't see your charms."

"It's more like…I didn't see theirs."

"Fair enough. You do not look like an innocent to me."

"What do I look like to you?"

He put his thumb on her chin. "A seductress."

"That's…almost sweet." She kissed his thumb. "Are you seduced?"

Utterly. He was ready to get on his knees and beg. He had waited long enough for this moment. He had waited forever to feel something like this.

This was different. Different than a lust that cared only for feeding itself. This was like the first time.

Oh, *Theos,* how he wished it was the first time. How he wished those other moments, those other women, those cold, selfish encounters, had not been. But he could not erase his past from reality. Only from his mind.

"I don't think we have as much to worry about as you might imagine."

"You don't?" she asked.

"No. I have always believed in making plans. When I decided to marry, I knew I would need to have the skills a husband is required to have to satisfy his wife. More than a teenage boy would need with a woman who was not even a lover. So I have done some reading. I am also gifted with singular focus. When I am in bed with you I will apply both my knowledge and my focus to you entirely, at the exclusion of everyone and everything else. A man who has had a lover every day for the past eighteen years, but only has a tenth of my focus and perfectionism could not come close to satisfying you as I will."

Her eyes darkened, irises shrinking to a gold line around a pool of black. Her breath shallow, the pulse at the base of her delicate throat pounding. Yes, she was a woman aroused. A woman who wanted this. Wanted him.

A virgin.

Strangely he found that revelation to be disturbing. A vague and unsettling parallel. Considering that he felt his very touch was a violation of her innocence. Emotional innocence was all he'd been betting on. It seemed especially disturbing, underlining the point, that she was innocent in this way, as well.

He was not. No matter how many years stood between him and those other women, him and that time in his father's house, he carried the evidence on his soul. Dirt that would never come clean.

And he had tried. He'd expected some sort of feeling of absolution. Sins washed white as snow when he'd helped to destroy the wicked empire his father had built. When he'd helped to free countless women and men from the trade. And yet, even when that was finished, he'd looked inside of himself and he'd still seen the monster.

There was nothing clean in him. Some stains stayed forever. And he had to be mindful of that. Of the fact that no matter how much had changed around him, not enough had changed in him.

But he wouldn't back out now. He couldn't. Not when she was looking at him like he was the best present she'd ever got.

Another testament to her innocence. Her naïveté. She didn't know what she was asking for. Didn't know the man that she was about to make love with. He *should* tell her. Who he was, where he was from. About all the life he'd lived before he'd walked through the wrought iron gates of the Holt Manor and became Ajax Kouros, leaving his real name, his life, his connections with Greece's most notorious drug and human trafficker far behind him.

He should tell her how he hadn't been a captive of that man, no, he was that man's son. He shared his genetics. He'd lived in the mansion, worn suits, driven cars, bought with money dripping with the blood of innocents.

No, he hadn't known better. But it didn't matter in the end. It was still what had created him.

And that night, he'd come face-to-face with a choice: embrace the monster, or leash him, shoving him down and moving forward, half a man, but a decent human being. He'd chosen to be decent.

But it didn't mean the monster wasn't there. It didn't mean it didn't prowl inside of him, waiting for a chance to escape and devour everything in its path. The monster who remembered what it was like to live only for yourself, to taste excess. He would kill it if he could. Instead, he'd spent years trying to choke it out, making it weak. Leaving it forgotten. Starving its appetites.

But tonight, it was just beneath his skin. Claws digging in, threatening to tear its way through his flesh. And he didn't want to put it back in the cage. Tonight he wanted to let the beast free. Wanted to sate that appetite.

No. He would not. It would be unthinkable.

"Do you think you can handle me?" he asked, putting his hands on her cheeks, looking at her eyes.

A smile curved her lips. "I was going to ask you the same question."

He hesitated, unsure of where she would want him to start. What he should do. Still, a part of him wanted to protect her. Give her something sweet and unchallenging. A few moments in bed to consummate the marriage, dispense with her virginity and his celibacy and move on.

But then there was the beast. And Ajax feared if he made

the wrong move he wouldn't be able to hold that part of himself back any longer.

Leah took the choice from him.

She kissed him, hard, deep, devouring, her tongue sliding against his, teeth scraping his bottom lip. Her fingers were forked through his hair, her body pressed hard against his.

He put one arm around her waist, and with the other he did what he'd been longing to do since…it felt like forever. It felt like a need that had been building in him long before he'd ever recognized it.

He cupped her breast, so soft, so incredibly sexy, sliding his thumb over her nipple. She arched into him, her soft flesh filling his palm. So perfect. So incredibly perfect. A fit he could only find with Leah.

Things were burning hot and fast, her hands creeping beneath the hem of his shirt, fingertips skimming over the muscles on his back, his stomach, his chest. This wasn't the sweet and easy first time he'd imagined.

And it felt like the first time for him, too. The first time he might have had.

But he couldn't stop to ask for something else. Not when this was what he really wanted. This moment of freedom. This moment of satisfied need in what amounted to a lifetime of self-denial.

She pulled away from him and stood back, her lips swollen, her eyes sultry, tempting. Then she reached behind herself and tugged the zipper on her dress.

"Stop," he said, his throat tight. "Let me."

She turned slowly, sweeping her hair to the side, exposing her back. He put his arm around her, his hand resting on her stomach. Then he lowered his head and kissed the back of her neck, resting his forehead there for a moment. He felt a shiver go through her body and she arched back, her bottom coming up against the hard ridge of his erection. He pulled her into his body even tighter, thrusting against her.

A raw sound escaped her lips. Passion. Need. Not fear. Everything he needed to keep going.

Although, he was so far gone now, he feared he was past the point of needing encouragement. He was lost in his desire, lost in the sensations coursing through his body, a body he never let make decisions. A body he denied pleasure on a daily basis.

He lifted his hand and gripped the tab on the zipper, drawing it down slowly, the fabric parting. He slid his hand down over the wedge of pale exposed skin, skimming his knuckles over her silken flesh. Then he lowered his head and kissed her, just between her shoulder blades.

"Oh, yes, Ajax."

"See? I think we'll muddle through."

She nodded, and he laughed. And in that moment, time seemed to freeze. He looked in her eyes, and saw a flash of the past. Not of the past at his father's house. The past in the offices at Holt. Leah looking at him, smiling, putting a piece of chocolate on his desk.

One he would eat later, though something in him felt it was wrong to do it. That it was wrong to encourage the growing connection between them. A connection that seemed to start at his chest, tendrils weaving through to the rest of him, slowly, unbidden.

Then, he'd turned away from it. He'd had to. But now...now he wouldn't look away.

He pushed the dress from her shoulders, letting it fall off her body, pooling at her feet. He could only stare. At her curves, highlighted by the black lace bra and panties.

Her small waist, the dramatic flare of her hips, the shape of her buttocks. He couldn't stop himself from putting his hand on her hip, from inching it around so that he could palm her ass. So perfect.

There was a beauty that radiated from her, so rare, so incredible, that he felt humbled by it. Shamed by it. He was not worthy to put his hands on her, and yet he couldn't resist the chance to.

"I want to touch you," he said, his voice so unlike his own. There was no control. There was no civility. There was barely any trace of the man left. It was more of a growl. More like a beast.

"Where?" she asked, her voice soft.

"Everywhere. And then I want to taste you. Everywhere."

"I like that promise."

"It's one I can keep."

He unhooked her bra and she tugged it down from her shoulders, tossing it aside. He wrapped his arm around her again, cupping her bare breasts, her skin so soft, nipple tight against his palm. His first time touching a woman this way. Need, shocking, hot, and like nothing he'd ever felt before, burst through him.

"I need to see you," he said, kissing the top of her shoulder. "I have waited for so long."

She turned to face him, eyes glistening. "So have I. Ajax... you don't know how long."

There was no shyness, no timidity in her gaze. And he looked his fill. He had never seen anything more beautiful than the sight of Leah, standing there, her breasts bared, raspberry nipples dark against her pale skin. He let his eyes travel farther down, to the little scrap of fabric that covered her most intimate place from his gaze.

"Take them off," he said, and this time, it was a growl.

She never took her eyes off his as she hooked her fingers in the sides of her panties and dragged them down her legs.

He looked at her, desire, desperation, clawing at his throat. He had just enough breath to issue a warning. "I'm about to skip some steps," he said.

He dropped to his knees, pressed a kiss to her stomach, just beneath her belly button. And lower. He was shaking, dying for his first taste of her. He wanted, needed, in a way he couldn't remember ever needing. It was visceral, as necessary as breathing.

He parted her thighs slightly, widening her stance, and covered her with his mouth, sliding his tongue through her slick folds, over the little bundle of her nerves he knew would bring her the most pleasure.

She gasped and bent forward, her hands clinging to his shoulders. And he continued to taste her, deeper, faster. He couldn't get enough of her. He never would. Her taste, the way she coated his tongue, the way she breathed his name, the way her nails cut into his skin, even with the fabric of his shirt as a buffer.

This was a first for him, something he'd never done. Because he had never cared about the satisfaction of the women in his father's house. They were prostitutes, and he had been taught to treat them in a certain way. Taught that their pleasure came from whatever they got in trade.

He shoved the thought aside and focused on Leah.

She filled his senses. Sustained him. How had he lived without this?

He gripped her hips and pressed her more firmly against his lips, lost in the act, lost in her.

"Ajax…" She said his name like a plea, like a prayer, and when her release broke over her, almost like a curse, her body trembling as he held her up, he rested his head against her thigh, trying to catch his breath, and she laced her fingers through his hair. The gesture was shockingly sweet, coming on the tail end of something so raw and uncontrolled, and yet it felt right.

His hands were shaking, so much that he found it hard to undo the buttons on his shirt. But Leah took over. Her hands left a trail of fire over his skin, testing him, pushing him to the limit, and when she cupped him, stroked him through his jeans, he caught her wrist and pulled her hand away.

"Careful," he said.

"What?"

"Too much."

It certainly hadn't been eighteen years since he'd had an orgasm, but in that time, he'd only had them alone. He had been convinced that he would have control, much in the same way he did with his own hand. That sex would feel familiar due to years of self-gratification.

But he had left out the variable.

The woman. His partner.

Leah was an active participant, and she wasn't keeping his pace. Wasn't letting things go down the path he'd imagined. Wasn't allowing him to keep to his plan.

She was forging her own, and bringing him with her.

"I like that you're on edge," she said, putting her hand against him again. "I like that you want me so much."

"Leah," he bit out.

"Yes." She sighed, squeezing him. "Say it again."

"Don't."

"Not that. My name."

"Leah," he said again, on a feral growl.

"I like it."

And he liked it, too. Too much to stop her, even though he should. Even though he should try to get control of the situation again. Control of his needs. He should be commanding this; he shouldn't be at her command.

"Stop touching me," he said. "Now."

She removed her hand from him, and he reached down and started to work his belt, undoing it and the button and zip on his pants, shoving them down his legs and kicking them aside.

"Not fair," she said. "I want to touch."

"No."

If she touched him it would be over. Not the sex. He wouldn't come. But he didn't know what he would do. If the fire got too hot. If the beast slipped its chains.

"Go into the bedroom," he said. Because he had to assert authority. He had to find his control. Hold it tight.

"Is that how we're going to play?"

He took her chin between his thumb and forefinger and dropped a light kiss on her lips. "If you want to play, *agape,* then you play by my rules. Now go to the bed and wait for me like a good girl."

He hadn't known it would be like this. Hadn't known he would be like this. But this, the demands, the orders, made for an easy reminder. An easy role to slip into that would help him maintain control.

A smile curved her lips, but he wasn't fooled. He saw the steel shining through. "Of course, darling."

She turned and walked away from him, giving her hips an extra sway, a show for his amusement. He reached down and squeezed his erection, sucking a sharp breath through his teeth.

"Hey," she said, turning and looking over her shoulder, her focus lowering to where his hand was wrapped around his shaft. "Not fair. If I can't touch, you can't."

He lowered his hand, and she continued on to the bed, sweeping the curtain to the room aside and climbing on, leaning back against the pillows, her arms draped to the sides. She was inviting. She was certainly not a *shy* virgin.

He walked over to the bed and stood at the side, and she rose up onto her knees, her eyes locked with his. She leaned in and pressed a kiss to his chest, and he wove his fingers through her hair. She moved lower, lips skimming his abs, blazing a trail farther down. Then her tongue flicked over the head of his arousal. The pleasure, the heat, seared through his skin, rocking him, threatening to destroy him. He tugged her hair, pulling her head backward.

"We're not playing like that, *agape,*" he said, his voice strained. "Not tonight."

"But you did it for me. I want to taste you."

"No. Not tonight." He was too close to the edge, his control too tenuous.

And his control was everything.

"What do you want then?"

"This." He joined her on the bed and dipped his head, sucking one pink nipple deep into his mouth and flicking his tongue over the tightened bud. He ran through the instructions he'd read on how to pleasure a woman this way, text swimming before his closed eyes, the need for concentration the perfect counterbalance for the ache in his body.

And she was the one shaking now, her fingers locked in his hair. This was what he could handle. This was what he wanted.

He turned his attention to the other breast, sucking, licking, until she was panting beneath him, little sounds of pleasure escaping her lips. He raised his head and kissed her, hard, and she returned it.

He could feel her desperation now, her need.

"Are you ready?" he asked. In this he would ask, because he knew for her there would be pain. And he didn't like that. Didn't relish it.

"Yes. Oh, yes, please now."

She parted her thighs and he settled between them taking himself in hand and pressing against the moist entrance to her body. Then he pulled back, replacing his erection with one finger, sliding it in slowly until she sighed.

She was so tight. So wet. And he nearly lost it then and there. He gritted his teeth and moved his finger within her, sliding his thumb over her clitoris.

"Good?" he asked.

"Yes."

"More?"

"Yes," she said.

He added a second, stretching her gently, working them in and out of her until he felt her internal muscles tighten around him. His stomach was so tight he could hardly breathe; he was aching with the need to be in her. To feel her around him there. To be connected to her.

He withdrew his fingers, positioning himself again. He could feel her heat, the slick wetness of her desire against the head of his arousal. She kissed his neck, the corner of his mouth, her hands moving over his back. Touching. Tempting. Testing.

He tightened his hands into fists around the sheet as he slid inside of her, inch by inch, slowly, excruciatingly so, but more for him than for her. He was lost. For one blinding moment his mind was clear of everything. Of his need for restraint, control.

There was only this. Only her body. Only the feeling of her around him.

He pushed in deep, thrusting hard, and she gasped, a little note of pain in the sound that brought him sharply back to the present.

"Okay?" he asked.

She nodded, biting her lip. He bent his head and kissed her. "If you're going to bite someone's lip," he said, "make it mine."

He didn't expect her to oblige him, but she did, pinning his lip tightly in her teeth. And the pain was just enough to take the edge off the pleasure, just enough to help him regain some of his control.

He thrust into her again, establishing a rhythm, her nails scraping against the bare skin of his back, his shoulders. Her touch inflaming, the pain anchoring, necessary.

"Harder," he bit out, gripping her thigh and tugging it up over his hip as he continued to ride her. Her hold on his shoulders deepened, her nails digging in enough that he was sure she had to be drawing blood. "Harder," he said again. And she obliged.

Every time he entered her, she arched into him until finally he felt her go stiff beneath him, a soundless scream on her lips, her warmth pulsing around him. And he let go. The rhythm forgotten, the steadiness gone. Only a blinding race to the finish remained as his blood roared in his ears, the strength of his release savaging him, tearing him to pieces inside and leaving them scattered, impossible to collect. Impossible to ever be whole again in the way he'd been before this. Before his orgasm.

Before Leah.

Somehow, in one wrenching moment, his wife had changed everything. And he felt nearly desperate to find a way to change it back.

CHAPTER NINE

LEAH'S WORLD WAS rocked. Completely. Ajax in theory was one thing. Ajax in reality was another thing entirely.

He had been firm, gentle sometimes, commanding, and OMG those years where his sexual activity had been dormant had clearly not affected him adversely. He knew about hot buttons on the female body that she'd never discovered on her own, and he knew how to do just the right things to them.

She could hardly breathe. What had it been, ten, twenty minutes since they'd parted? Since her orgasm had shattered her? Or maybe it had been two hours. Or thirty seconds. She honestly had no idea.

Ajax rolled into a sitting position, his back to her, his muscular, *perfect* back, to her. She reached out and traced her fingers over the lines on his back.

Ajax's body was sculpted, well-defined, without a spare ounce of flesh anywhere. Almost like he worked out to the point of punishing himself. Or to the point of exhaustion so he couldn't want anymore. She knew a little something about that. If she was faced with the choice of rolling around, tangled up in her sheets, dying of sexual frustration brought about by Ajax fantasies, she often opted to go and run on the treadmill.

When she didn't opt for a shower to uh…alleviate things in a different way altogether.

Maybe he would shower with her later. That was an optimistic thought.

He stood and she cocked her head to the side, taking in the view. Oh, the view. She'd admired that view many times. When it was covered in denim, or black, well-fitted dress pants. But naked? Oh, that was its own pleasure. She would happily buy tickets to this show.

"Where are you going?" she asked, when he started to move away from the bed.

"I have some work to do," he said, bending down and picking up his pants from the floor, tugging them up, covering her peep show.

"What? You have...work? What kind of work could you possibly have to do after...after that?" Oh, no, she sounded so...needy. So raw and exposed. But she'd had to let her guard down for that, to be with him that way.

And she hadn't had a chance to protect herself again. Like she'd just shed her scales, leaving behind new, shiny skin that was tender to the touch. To Ajax's coldness.

He turned, the muscles in his stomach rippling. "The world didn't stop turning just because we had sex."

She could only stare at him, words frozen on her lips. Her world had stopped. It had been rocked, in fact, she'd just thought that it'd been rocked; and it turned out everything was going on just fine in Ajax land. No big deal. He had work.

Screw that.

"Well, I think the world should stop for a second," she said. "This is supposed to be a real marriage...this is supposed to be our honeymoon. I know we're trying to make it look like things are good for the press, but you said this was a forever kind of thing. And...and that means you need to get back here and start acting like a husband."

"I just acted my part," he said. "Were you not satisfied?"

"I am not satisfied," she hissed, sitting up, tugging the covers over her breasts.

"Your screams during your multiple orgasms tell a different story."

"You… You… That was uncalled-for. And rude. And anyway, sexual satisfaction and my satisfaction with this moment are not inextricably linked!"

"This is a real marriage, *agape,* as I said it would be. I was in your bed tonight as you requested, but what happens after that, that's up to me."

"This isn't how marriage is," she said, her throat closing on the last word, making it sound choked. Betraying her emotion. What was wrong with her? Her armor wasn't protecting her now. She was breaking apart behind the layer of protection she counted on. The damage coming from the inside out.

"It's how *our* marriage is."

He turned and walked through the curtain, down into the living area, and she just sat there, her knees drawn up to her chest, a shiver, a chill, working its way through her body.

For her, sex had changed everything. And it seemed to have changed things for him, too. But he didn't feel closer to her. It didn't make him want to hold her or be near her.

She'd given him her body. Let him run his hands over her bare skin, let him *into* her body.

She had given him absolutely everything. And it still hadn't made him want her. It had only made him want to put her at a greater distance.

And the very last bit of fantasy, the last little shaft of light in the darkness, the hope that she hadn't realized still lived inside of her, that someday he would feel something for her, was snuffed out.

She was very careful to avoid Ajax for as long as possible the next day. When she woke up, early the next morning, he was asleep on the couch. She had to fight the urge to go to him and cover him with a blanket, or smooth his hair back from his forehead, or try to move him into a more comfortable position.

He'd clearly fallen asleep while working, half sitting up, his laptop on the table in front of him, his neck turned at an angle that looked the opposite of comfortable.

But it worked out, because his obviously exhausted state allowed her to sneak out undetected. She spent the day wandering around the private beaches and swimming, stopping at the bar for a fruity drink and some lunch.

Yes, for being a small, exclusive island, there were a lot of ways and places to avoid her new husband, and to get a grip on what had happened between them last night. Try to figure out a way to rebuild the walls inside.

But she didn't know how to do that. Didn't know how to protect herself when it felt like he was in her.

She sighed and let her wrap drop around her ankles. Then she started to half jog down to the waves. She stopped, adjusted her bikini top and rethought the jogging. There was not enough support in that itty-bitty red top for that much bouncing up and down.

"How are you doing?"

She turned around, midadjust, her hand stuffed down her top, and saw Ajax. She slowly removed her hand and tried not to die of embarrassment. "Morning," she said.

"I asked how you were."

"I don't know… How are you? You were practically a virgin, and don't virgins get all emotional after sex?"

"Leah, I'm being serious."

"So am I."

He shrugged his broad shoulders, his loose white shirt tightening across his chest. "Fine."

"Oh, yeah, good. Me, too. Fine. Totally fine. I'm glad you're fine because I'd hate to feel all guilty over any wounded virtue."

"I haven't got any."

"So you've said."

"And you?"

"My wounded virtue? Fine. Fine."

"That's what I was asking about."

"Okay," she said, putting her hands up. "I'm not fine. I don't want you sleeping on the couch."

"Why?"

"Because it feels wrong. Don't you think a married couple should share a bed?"

"Often in history married couples haven't."

"So? Often in history people died of dysentery, but that's not really a trend I want to continue."

"You don't know what it will be like…to spend so much time with me. Perhaps you should worry about something other than sharing a bed all night. Like if you'll be able to stand having breakfast with me in the morning."

"Or maybe, since it's our honeymoon, we see how much of each other we can stand. Why not have a little immersion therapy?"

"Why not keep us both from *needing* therapy?"

"Ajax, why don't you want to share a bed with me?"

"It's not what I do, Leah."

"You admitted to me you hadn't done anything like this in a long time, so how is it you have formed opinions on how you should be in this situation?" She looked out at the water, trying not to cry or do anything similarly humiliating. Like smacking him over the head. "Would you have shared a bed with Rachel?"

"No," he said, his voice rough.

"But I thought you loved her."

"I didn't, Leah, obviously."

The admission stunned her, left her feeling hollow. "What's that supposed to mean? You've been telling me all this time that you loved her. You weren't with another woman from the time you met her."

He put his hands on his head. "None of this ever had anything to do with her. I made a plan. I decided marrying her would be the best thing for my life, marrying into the Holt fam-

ily would be the best thing for my life, and feelings…followed."
He dropped his hands back down to his sides, curled them into
fists. "But I have hardly thought of her since our marriage, and
I would be shocked if you could find a man who would think
of her, when he had you, naked and underneath him."

His voice got deeper, rougher, the light in his eyes changing.

"Well…then," she said. "I guess there's…that."

"You do not like the thought of her with me," he said.

"Brilliant observation there, Sherlock, I really don't."

"Why?"

"Well, answer me this, Ajax, and whatever the answer is,
make it honest. What do you think about another man touching me? Kissing me like you did? Touching my breasts the
way you did."

A muscle in Ajax's jaw jumped. "I think…I think I would
have to kill him. And when I say that, I don't say it lightly. Or
metaphorically."

She swallowed. "Oh." She believed him. Somehow, she
believed him. "Ajax…who were you before you came to our
home? Before you came to work for my father?"

"This discussion is not…necessary. I don't…"

"You told me that last night. As if by keeping it from me
you were protecting me, but honestly? Real honesty here, not
protecting myself, not putting on a happy face. Not hiding
tears. You destroyed me. Your reaction to what happened between us. Leaving me like you did. You can't just pretend that
by closing yourself down and giving me nothing you won't be
hurting me."

"Leah, you don't know what you're asking."

"No, I don't. So tell me. It hardly seems fair. You've known
me most of my life. You know my family. You saw me all
through my hideous awkward stage, which, in my opinion,
gives you way too much power. I know you didn't just appear
one day. I know you got your scars from somewhere. Tell me
so I understand."

"You don't want to understand."

"I do."

"No." He turned, his expression fierce. "I'm not going to stand here on a beach with you in that ridiculous bikini and tell you all the sordid details of my life."

She let out a growl and reached behind her, undoing one of the ties on her bikini. Then she yanked off the top and threw it into the sand. "There. Half the ridiculous bikini is gone. So tell me part of the story." She waved her hand over her midsection. "Half, even. You could tell me half."

He looked around them, then back at her. "What the hell are you doing?"

"My bikini was a problem. I have removed the problem. Half of it anyway. Tell me."

"You can't just…stand there like that."

She put her hands on her hips, anger, adrenaline, coursing through her. Because her defenses weren't holding. They weren't rebuilding. The only other option was to get him to bare himself, too. And if she had to stand there, half-naked to get him to do it, it was a small trade.

"Can. Am. Tell."

Ajax sucked in a sharp breath, his eyes glued, no matter how hard he tried to get them not to be, to Leah's breasts. She pushed him. Brought him to the brink, so that the monster tugged at his chain, begging to be released. And if he wasn't careful, the chains would break completely.

He could do this. She was testing him, and he wouldn't fail.

"You don't want to know this, Leah. This is…the kind of darkness you've never seen."

"I can handle your darkness, Ajax," she said, whiskey eyes burning into his.

The look in his eyes was that of a man ready to go into the torture chamber. "I don't want you to have to handle it."

"Tough. I married you. That means it concerns me. I'm not a child. I'm not a sheltered flower… Ajax, my whole life has been lived in front of the world. I have had total strangers leave the most hideous comments about me on blogs, in news stories, all because…because when you have any kind of public face, whether you want it or not, people feel like they own you. And that showed me a lot about people. A lot of really horrible things about people. So maybe to you I seem innocent or unaffected, but the simple truth is that I've seen more than you think. You can trust me with your story. With your darkness. I won't run."

"But maybe you should."

"I won't."

He paused for a moment, the words sticking in his throat. "My father was…is, I imagine, I doubt he's changed his name… Nikola Kouklakis. And no, we don't share a name. No, it is not by accident. But by my design."

He could see her thinking, could see her processing, wondering where she'd heard the name.

"He is a criminal. The most notorious criminal in Athens. One of the worst in the world. Doubtless you've heard his name on the news. He is a drug lord and human trafficker, and I was born and raised in his compound. My mother was never there. I don't even know who she is. I was raised by my father, the most violent, reviled man in Greece. And before I left, I nearly became him. It's what I was being groomed for. To take the place of a man who sold drugs and women. And do you know what, Leah? I would have. I could have."

She shook her head, her eyes glittering. "No, Ajax, you couldn't have."

"Yes, Leah, I could have. Why do you think it's so important I keep control? Why do you think I have to plan everything, keep my eyes on the prize ahead. Because if I don't…greed, corruption, murder, all of that is in my blood. It's who I am. Bred into me, raised into me. Nature or nurture? Doesn't matter, I have both on the side of darkness, and it is all still in me. If I don't keep it chained, if I don't keep it under control…."

"That's ridiculous, Ajax. You aren't a criminal any more than I am."

"If you run through the alleyways in the middle of the city, you make two right turns, then pass two buildings. At a third, you take a left. You knock on the door, and someone answers, usually a kid. Say whatever the word of the night is, and they show you to the back. They open up your backpack, inspect the packages. You take the money, and you go home." He swallowed. "You have to know it like that. Memorize it. Because you make the trip in the dark. And it's scary, especially when you're a little kid. So you need to know it. Know what to do, know what to say. And you have to be damn fast so you don't wind up with a slit throat. Or worse."

"What's worse?" she asked, her voice hoarse.

"Being sold. Trust me. It's worse. People who want to buy boys…it's not for anything good." He looked at her, at the horror etched onto her lovely face. "I am a drug runner. Is that not criminal activity?"

"You were a mule. A child."

"Call it what you will, there was an age when I knew what I was doing and when I continued to do it. Family business and all." He thought back, to the opulent mansion on the hill, overlooking the city. To the halls, filled with people, women, who were like wraiths, hollow eyed and desperate. Hungry looking. Willing to sell any and everything for a taste of their drug of choice.

"It is the most hideous business," he said. "Drugs turn people into ghosts. They steal everything vital from them. Everything alive. The color goes from them. They have one drive, and one drive only—the next fix. And they will sacrifice anything to get it. We—my father, me—we capitalized on that."

"Not you. You were a child."

"I lived in the mansion. I wore custom suits bought with that money."

"Yes, but you aren't there now."

"Stop trying to excuse it. I ran drugs when I was a boy, but I took them as a teenager. And I used the women who were addicted to them. I suspect…" He hesitated. "I have long suspected that Alexios Christofides was the child of a prostitute who lived in my father's compound. I don't know it for sure… but he hates me, and it's with enough ferocity that I know it goes beyond business."

"But you wouldn't have done anything to him, you were a boy…you."

"I was part of the problem. Do you want to know how I lost my virginity, Leah? To a prostitute. Not the kind that were kidnapped and sold, one of the ones who hung around waiting for her favored poison." She wanted to close her eyes. To block out his face, to block out the words, as the pieces of the puzzle that was Ajax Kouros came together. As the boy she'd cared for, the man who stood before her, merged into one. Merged with this new truth. "I traded her. She took my virginity, I gave her an ounce of cocaine. Generous, really. And that's not all. That's not everything. It's not even close. You can't begin to understand it. I was a boy, wandering around a massive mansion filled with vice, and none of it was locked to me. Some days I didn't eat, because no one prepared food for me. It was there, but do you think anyone spared me a thought? Not until I learned where the power was in the little class system my father built for himself. Sex and drugs."

"I don't… I didn't…"

"You didn't imagine it was that, did you? Because you're so…lucky to have been given what you were given. And I have spoiled it now. I shouldn't have tried to make you understand. I should not have forced this on you."

A flash went before his mind. A girl crying. Her dress torn. A piece of fabric in his hand. Proof *he* had done it. That her tears were his fault. That her fear was because of him. And clarity from the haze of drugs his father had given him, just enough clarity, to look up and into the mirror that hung on the wall in the bedroom and see the monster. And recognize that it was him.

"I asked."

"Cover yourself," he said, his voice rough.

"Why?"

"Because I…I can't think with you standing there like that." With his past bleeding into his present. The darkness covering all the beautiful light Leah had given him last night.

"Maybe you don't need to think."

She took a step toward him and he reached out and grabbed her wrist. "Did you hear nothing of what I just told you? Of who I am?"

"The son of a violent horrible criminal. And maybe if I hadn't known you for most of my life, maybe it would affect me. But I have seen your actions, Ajax, for years. I watched you work your way from the doing grounds work, to being an assistant to my father. Then, a trusted advisor before you were eighteen. I saw how my father believed in you, sent you to school, brought you on as an intern at Holt. I saw his faith in you, and I saw you never disappoint that faith. And my sister…you never laid a hand on her. Never hurt her. You wanted to honor her with marriage vows. And me. A silly kid who followed you around and talked about candy…you listened to me. No, Ajax, when I look at you I don't see a monster."

"You've never seen me without my plan. My control."

"Sure I have. Our wedding day."

She leaned in, her lips brushing his, and he leaned back. "Not now." He could tell her. He could tell her what it looked like when he really lost control. Or he could show her.

He was tempted. To lay her down in the sand and claim her, hard, fast, taking and satisfying the never-ending hunger in him. To try to fill the blackness with her light.

But he would not. Because if he let it go, even for a moment, with her, he might never get it back. Might never be able to subdue it, subdue himself, again.

"Don't," he bit out.

"Why?"

For one moment, his mind was moving too fast, his blood flowing too hot to formulate an answer. And then she reached out and put her palm flat on his chest, the heat and fire that assaulted him nearly too much to endure.

And he was pulling her against him, breasts crushed against his chest, his mouth crushed against hers. And he needed. Blind need, deeper, more all-consuming than anything had ever been.

Like the craving for a drug. Altering, impossible to resist. It pushed him to the edge, held him there, threatening to send him over. Into the abyss. He wanted to jump. Wanted to follow this desire straight to hell and drag her with him if he had to, so long as he could get what he needed.

So long as he could get his fix.

He pulled back, his chest rising and falling with each harsh breath. He started to speak but he couldn't form any words. So he just turned and left her there, on the beach, in nothing but her bikini bottoms.

And for the first time in his memory, he had no plan.

CHAPTER TEN

AJAX SAT AT the foot of the bed, a scarf stretched between his fists. He'd been thinking, all afternoon and until the sun went down, about what he would do with Leah. What he could do with her. She was his wife—there was no getting around that. A wife he'd promised to make a marriage with…but when she touched him it all went blank.

He couldn't see the path up ahead anymore. All he could see was those whiskey-colored eyes. Eyes that had tested him years ago. Had enticed him into something he hadn't identified. Something he'd forced himself to turn away from. And now, he was bewitched by them again. And couldn't hold on to his control. He could only see her.

The problems really started when she touched him. It had to stop.

If he could just keep some of the control. If he could take the variables away and have all the power. All the power and Leah's naked body, spread out before him. To take pleasure in, to give pleasure to.

One time with her and he was on his way to obsession.

She'd asked him if he would have shared Rachel's bed. He was pretty certain he'd lied. That he would have shared Rachel's bed because it was something a husband did with a wife.

And because Rachel wouldn't have challenged his control in the same way that Leah did. He had always known that.

Leah walked in the front door of the villa, dressed in her

swimsuit and cover-up, and the truth hit him full on. He had always known it would be like this. That Leah was the one who would wake up the monster.

She tugged at the flowing fabric on the cover-up, stretching it over her breasts. He'd been half hoping she would come through wearing nothing but bikini bottoms but he was disappointed on that front.

Was he disappointed? Yes. No point in pretending he didn't want her. He did. More than he could remember wanting anything or anyone. The acquisition of Holt seemed like nothing now, not compared to the need to join his body to Leah's.

She kept comparing his celibacy to her innocence. As if it united them somehow. As if they shared something. But she did not share in his darkness.

They were nothing alike. And she didn't know what she was tempting.

And if he had his way, she never would.

He wrapped the scarf around his fist and tugged it so that it was taut, watching her through the curtain as she approached the bed, her hips swaying gently, each step she took tightening the desire in his stomach further.

"Where have you been?" he asked.

"And you care why?"

"I'm your husband," he said, the words scraping his throat raw.

"Oh, really. Well, you can't just be my husband when it suits you, Ajax. You can't shove me away on the beach and walk away then expect that you get to know the details of my whereabouts."

"If something had happened to you?"

"I lived the first twenty-three years of my life without you in my pocket, I'm pretty sure I can handle the next twenty-three without you there, too."

"Tell me, Leah, knowing everything you know about me—"

he wrapped the scarf around his fist again, drawing his hands more tightly together "—do you still want me?"

She lifted her chin. "Yes."

"Tell me," he said, "exactly what you want from me."

"I already told you."

"Tell me again," he said. "Restate your terms." He had to know. He had to hear it again.

"You. In my bed. Children," she said, adding more now, "support of my business. The expansion of Leah's Lollies should be a priority."

He pulled his fists as far from each other as he could, the fabric straining between them. "Done."

"And what has this deal cost me? My soul?"

"I don't want your soul, darling girl, I want your body."

"I offered it. Freely."

"On my terms."

"And what," she asked, her voice breathy, "are your terms?"

"You can't touch me during sex."

"That's impossible," she said.

"No, it's not. When you touch me, when you push me too far too fast, I start to lose control, and that is unacceptable."

"And you have a solution?"

"You said you could handle my darkness." He stood from his position on the bed, the scarf still wrapped around his hands.

Her eyes fell to the scarf and shock flickered in the golden depths. Then, she raised her gaze to meet his, her tongue darting out slowly to moisten her lips. "Are you offering to show me the darkness?"

"No," he said, his voice rough, "I aim to protect you from it."

"How?"

"I need control."

"How much?"

"All of it. Can you give me that? In bed, I need all of the control."

Leah's heart thundered in her head, her hands shaking, her

entire body shaking, from the inside out. She felt like she might really be in over her head. Like she might have miscalculated. For the first time, when she looked at Ajax, she felt like she was looking at a stranger.

"Tell me what you want to do," she said, knowing instinctively what it was he wanted. What he needed.

"I want to tie your hands."

"And then what?"

"I'm going to pleasure you until you can't think straight. Until you can't string together a sentence. And then…and then I want to part your legs and lose myself in you."

He was a stranger now. This raw, sexual part of him was something she'd never seen before. And it hit her, on the heels of the first thought, that this raw, sexual part of him was probably something no one but her had ever seen.

That it was probably something he'd never experienced, not when what he'd spoken of had been inexperienced couplings with prostitutes.

And she'd caused it to emerge.

Ajax was her dearest fantasy, her longest-held desire. He'd broken her heart, piece by piece for most of her life. With his obliviousness to her as a woman. The attention he gave to her sister. His engagement to her sister. His staunch refusal to show her any affection, any romance in their marriage.

And so right now, the need to have all of his attention focused on her, to be at his mercy, to be the subject of his dominance, was an answer to a fantasy that she couldn't say no to.

Because in that moment, she saw it clearly. His need for the ties was a concession to her power. To her ability to shake his control.

She recognized the power in his need for her to submit.

No, Ajax would never love her. The disconnect between the man he was and the man she'd imagined him to be was a chasm so wide there was no bridge that could cross it.

But she could have this. Enjoy this. Why not? Why not at

least get something out of this stupid obsession? These feelings that had done so much to define her life.

It felt like he owed her. In so many ways.

If she couldn't have it all, if he couldn't be the man she wanted, then maybe she could have this. She would have this. She would let him have total control, total command of her body, of her pleasure. She would have to stop protecting herself so much. Because there was no way to take everything he was giving if she was hiding behind a wall.

The reality that he couldn't love her. That she shouldn't love him…it should be protection enough.

She would take the pleasure he gave and she would keep it for herself.

She held her hands out in front of her. "Take me," she said.

A dark light, like a black flame, flared in his eyes. He unwound the length of silk from his fists, slowly, achingly so. Then he started wrapping it around her wrists. Slow. Sensual. He made it tight, made it so she couldn't move her hands. But she wanted the game. She didn't need freedom. Didn't want it. Not when captivity meant this.

"Tell me again," he said, his hands moving, strong and sure, securing the knot.

"Take me."

"Because?"

"Because I want you." She knew he needed to hear that, even if she didn't know why.

"On the bed," he bit out.

She obeyed, sitting on the edge, her bound hands in her lap. He stroked her face with the back of his hand, along her jaw, slow, sweet. Possessive.

He moved his hands to the knot of her bikini top, and untied it in one deft motion before removing her bathing suit wrap, letting it fall to her waist, along with the top of her swimsuit.

She was bare to him again, but instead of looking shocked, he looked hungry.

"Do you want to see the sort of thing a man who hasn't had sex in eighteen years is capable of?" he asked, his voice rough. "Do you want to see all that innocence you thought I had?"

And she knew he was going to make her pay for her comments on the beach. Make her pay in the best possible way. He lowered his head and drew her nipple deep into his mouth, sucking hard, and just like that, she couldn't think. Couldn't breathe.

She wanted to close her eyes, to sink into oblivion where there was only this, this pleasure, this feeling that ran deep and hot. But she forced her eyes to stay open, forced herself to look at him. To see Ajax, her dearest, most long-held fantasy, pleasuring her like this.

But he wasn't done. He abandoned her breasts and tugged her bathing suit cover down her thighs, getting onto his knees before her. Then he took her bikini bottoms and undid the ties, sending the scrap of fabric to join her wrap on the floor.

"Open your legs," he said.

And she was powerless to do anything but obey.

He settled between her thighs, pressing a kiss to her sensitive skin. The first touch of his tongue was like fire, white heat licking along her veins, a gasp catching in her throat.

"Lie back," he said, commanding, "and put your hands over your head."

She followed his orders, putting her hands over her head, her legs dangling over the bed. Then he gripped her legs and hooked them over his shoulders, pulling her against his mouth. The onslaught of sensation, of pleasure ripped through her. She was desperate to touch him, but she couldn't, her hands held captive, just as he held her soul captive.

Everything in her was poised on the brink, waiting for release, sobbing for it, desperate for it.

He shifted and started to pleasure her with his hands as well as his lips and tongue, sliding a finger inside her, sending a shock wave through her. She was close, so close. And every time she would get ready to go over the edge, he would pull back, just enough, before starting again, pushing her higher each time.

"Ajax…I can't. I can't…"

"Yes, you can," he said, sliding the flat of his tongue against her in time with the thrust of his fingers.

She rocked against him, trying to get herself the rest of the way there.

Then he moved away from her, leaving her buzzing and unsatisfied. "Not yet," he said, his hands going to the buckle on his pants.

She was dying. She needed to touch him, to taste him. And she knew he wouldn't let her.

He worked the belt through the loops slowly, then the button on the slacks, and the zipper. He tugged his shirt off over his head before shoving his slacks and underwear down lean hips, leaving him completely naked for her enjoyment.

Except she couldn't touch him. Dammit. She was desperate, and she had a feeling he was enjoying it.

So much for feeling powerful. But, while she didn't feel like she was in control, she definitely felt turned on. A good-enough quality of turned on, with the promise of a big-enough release that she was okay with feeling out of control.

In fact, part of her, a part of her she hadn't known existed, relished it.

"Do you approve?" he asked.

"More than," she said, sounding all breathless and shaky.

"Are you ready?"

"Not yet. I want to…I want to taste you," she said, her eyes on his erection.

"No. Sorry, *agape*. That's against the rules."

"I want to break the rules," she said.

"You will follow the rules, or I won't allow you to come," he said, his tone hard.

Her breath caught. "Oh."

"Will you be good?"

"Yes," she said, swallowing hard, her stomach tightening.

She noticed his hands didn't shake quite so much as they had last time when he joined her on the bed. His fingertips grazed her cheekbones, the gesture surprisingly gentle considering the game they were playing.

He pulled her up all the way onto the bed, strong arms locked around her, holding her tight. She inhaled deeply. She was surrounded by Ajax, and she had never felt so at peace. Everything from before, the bindings on her wrists, melted away for one fleeting moment.

And then he was poised over her, her arms above her head, thrusting her breasts toward his lips. And he made the most of it, pleasure arrowing from her nipples down to the apex of her thighs.

"Now," she said.

"No," he said, "that's not how this works." He pressed his length against her slick folds, sliding it back and forth. She gasped, arching into him.

"Please."

"That's better." He thrust his hips against her, the contact on her clitoris just right.

"Please," she said again, knowing that if she made a command, he would only deny her again.

He pressed the head of his erection against the entrance to her body and pushed inside her slowly. Tears stung her eyes, tears of relief. She needed him. Needed the release.

And then she was caught up completely, drowning in his kisses, in the rhythm of his body moving against hers. Her blood was roaring in her ears, pleasure building in her, so much, too much. She didn't think she could survive it.

"Please," she whispered again, the word barely making a sound on her lips.

He thrust into her one last time, stiffening above her, his arousal pulsing inside of her as he spent himself, his orgasm taking him over at the same moment hers broke through her and dragged her under.

When she came back to herself, her hands were still over her head, her arms starting to fall asleep. And so was she.

"Would you?" she asked, lifting her bound hands.

He sat up quickly, untied her, then he stood. He looked...she couldn't even quite put a word to it. Haunted maybe. Scared.

"I have work to do," he said, an echo of last night. "I'll join you when I'm finished."

Leah lay back down, rubbing her wrists, watching him walk naked down into the living area. He sat on the couch that way, his forearms resting on his legs.

And that was when she realized that as much as he'd been demanding of her, as out of her element as she was, Ajax was no better off.

Ajax had neatly severed his past from the man he'd become. All of the years she'd known him, she'd never seen his darkness.

She'd seen drive. Intelligence. Hunger. She just hadn't realized what had spurred the drive. That he'd been running, not just toward something, but from something.

From the darkness.

And she saw it now. Saw it in his eyes. And she was worried that he was getting too tired to keep running. She wanted to throw her armor onto him. To strip herself bare so she could protect him from it.

But she honestly had no idea how to hold the darkness at bay.

CHAPTER ELEVEN

THE HONEYMOON WENT by too quickly. She and Ajax were together every night. Every night, he bound her wrists, and every night he showed her a world of pleasure she hadn't imagined possible.

But they weren't closer during the day. Not any closer at all. In fact, she felt more distant from him than she ever had before.

During the day.

She closed her eyes as the plane touched down on the tarmac in New York. And she saw flashes of their time together in St. Lucia.

Her hands bound to the bedpost, her back to him. Candles the only light in the room. He'd skimmed his hand over her back, gripped her hips before thrusting in deep. And his voice…so desperate, so rough, in her ear, telling her how good it felt, words in broken Greek, some of which she'd never heard before.

She opened her eyes and looked out the window. It was cold and gray out there. Gray runway, gray skyline, gray sky.

"Good to be back," she said, waiting for the plane to stop before she stood up and stretched.

"You sound so enthused," he said.

"I am." She wasn't.

This was weird. She felt like she was talking to a stranger. A cold, detached stranger, not the man she'd had hot, erotic sex with all night, every night, for the past week. He was her lover, her only lover. There was no mistaking him. There could have been no other man with her those nights. And yet…and yet the Ajax sitting in front of her, all cool and calm and… bored, wasn't that man.

He wasn't the man brought to the edge by her body. By their conversation.

She wanted to touch him. But she wasn't allowed to.

Her fingers curled into fists at her side. It wasn't so much his command that she was obeying, but her self-control she was testing.

She didn't want to be enslaved to her need for him. She knew this wasn't going to be a great love match. More and more, she questioned whether or not he could actually love.

Because she was seeing parts of him, glimpses into his soul, that frightened her now.

Always, Ajax had been a constant presence in her life. Serious, studious, kind. Now he was her husband, and as her husband he was distant, angry. As her lover he was dominant, generous, sexy. And as a man…she wondered if she knew who he was at all. If the person she'd always known was nothing more than an illusion, than a careful facade he'd put on as a scared, runaway boy from the kind of past she couldn't have ever imagined.

As a girl, she hadn't seen it. She'd been blinded by his physical beauty, by his careful kindness to her. As a teenager, it had been those small smiles. The accepting of her gifts, that had held her in thrall. He hadn't said anything about his past, and she hadn't asked. She'd filled in the blanks, seen what she'd wanted to see. Thought what she'd wanted to think about him.

But nowhere in there had she imagined he would look at her with flat, black eyes. So closed off. So emotionless.

Never had she imagined him binding her hands and having sex with her. It was really the best way to describe it. They didn't make love. Ajax was demanding, and in terms of the physical, he gave her everything. But his eyes were hollow. He held himself back from her.

There was something about being tied up that she liked. His dominance was arousing, his skill was wonderful. And if it had been a game, nothing more than a power play between lovers, she wouldn't have had a complaint.

But Ajax was using it for something else. Using it to keep control. To hold himself at a distance.

She wasn't an equal in it. Wasn't able to give back.

Like the conversations they'd had when she'd been a teenager. Only this was their bodies. He was doing all the talking, all the work. But her hands were tied. Literally.

He wasn't letting her give. Wasn't letting her add herself to the mix. It was all him. All what he wanted, even though what he seemed to want was to give her endless, blinding orgasms, which seemed sort of petty and stupid to have an issue with, but it was the principle.

She'd never been less sure of anything in her life. She was married to Ajax, only to discover she didn't know him. To have the security of fantasy and her notion of love ripped away from her, when she was bound to him for life.

She really felt like she needed a drink.

Although, since she'd been having unprotected sex with Ajax for a week, maybe she shouldn't. Oh, jeez, that had to stop. Yes, she wanted children and she knew he did, too, but honestly, she was so messed up at the moment it just wasn't a very good idea.

Her phone pinged, and she looked down at the new message that was displayed on the screen. "Oh, Ajax, I have to stop by the store. Do you mind?"

He lifted one shoulder. "If it's an emergency, of course we should go."

The little show of support made her feel not quite so alone. "It's not really an emergency—my manager just wants me to check something out, but...I appreciate it."

"Of course. I'm investing in this company, so I need to make sure everything is running well."

Ouch. "Right. Of course."

She might not love him, but he was her lover, and she wished they had a little something personal between them. She wasn't just his lover, either, she was his wife. Lifelong family...acquaintance. Up until the past few weeks she would have called him a friend, but friends *knew* each other. They only knew each other in the biblical sense. And even then, that was only provided she followed his rules.

There had been a time in her life when she'd imagined that being with Ajax would solve all of her problems. Instead, he'd just introduced her to a whole new set of them she hadn't even known existed.

Leah's Lollies was a pop of color in the middle of the city. The floor was set up like a game board, brightly colored squares leading you down different paths. There was the road to the candy cane forest, which boasted huge candy canes spread around like trees, dusted in crystal. Every sort of mint was there. And then there was chocolate cove, with chocolate sculptures that were rotated out every season, and at least three hundred varieties of chocolate candy.

It was the lightest, frothiest excess Ajax had ever seen. And in some ways, he found it refreshing. He was all too familiar with the dark side of human appetites.

A little sugar seemed harmless in comparison.

As soon as they'd walked in, Leah had scurried to the back to speak to the manager, leaving Ajax standing in the middle of the fruit patch, where all the fruity treats lived. A girl, no older than sixteen, approached, wearing a white-and-red-striped uniform and an overdone smile.

"Welcome to Leah's. Lolly?" She held up a small lollypop that matched her uniform.

"No."

She looked a little bit crestfallen. But he wasn't a candy person. Except when Leah had left him candy. He'd always eaten that because he hadn't wanted to hurt her feelings.

Something he'd done constantly since their marriage, he was sure of that.

"Actually," he said, "No lollypop, but…do you have a red hard candy?"

"Tons. Cinnamon or fruity?"

"Fruity."

"Over this way."

Leah's candy expert helped him pick a bag of small red, round candies. Cherry. They reminded him of her. Of her red lips. The color they'd been the first time he'd kissed her for a reason other than show. The first time he'd kissed them just because he wanted to.

And they reminded him of her bikini. The one she'd worn the first night they'd made love.

Leah appeared a few moments after he'd paid for the candy and stuck the bag in his jacket pocket.

"Did you get bored?" she asked.

"How could anyone get bored in here?"

"I feel the same way," she said, a dreamy smile on her face. "I think my favorite store is the one in France, though. I'm test-driving a bakery. You should see all the macaroons set out every day. In every color you can possibly imagine. So far they've sold out by midday every day."

Leah's expression took on a dreamy quality, her enthusiasm obvious. Enviable.

He wondered what it must be like to love something so much. To have so much passion for your work, for anything in life.

He didn't know. He would never know. The nature of things, of himself, required that he keep too much of himself chained. Passion was very much in chains.

Except when you're with Leah. Then it's her in chains.

Chains or a silk scarf. That was passion tugging at its leash, getting close, but not getting free. A dangerous, dangerous game, but one he couldn't bring himself to give up. And not because of their agreement. Not because they both wanted children.

But because he craved the taste of her. The feel of her.

So deadly. So close to the edge. And yet, he couldn't stop himself. He didn't even want to. Leah had always had a way in. She had always mattered to him. And that foothold she'd made in his soul, early on, was now threatening to be the undoing of all of his efforts.

Was threatening to pull him back into darkness. A man who was a slave to his passions. A man who barely deserved life, much less the soft, sweet touch of Leah's hands.

The man he feared most.

At least during the day he could put things back to normal. At least with her wrists bound he had some form of control. At least the safeguards were holding.

He thought about the bag of cherry candies in his pocket and wondered what he was thinking. Wondered why he'd bought them.

Then he pushed the thought to the side. He would worry about it later. Everything was fine. His barriers were firmly in place. It was the perfect arrangement, really. He had Leah, beautiful—how had he ever missed how beautiful?— exciting Leah, in his bed every night. He had a wife by his side, one who understood his devotion to his work and was just as devoted to her own. One who made it possible for him to acquire Holt. One to keep his competitor well and truly foiled. Yes, things were absolutely perfect.

"Ready to go?" he asked, already thinking of how he would tie her hands tonight. How he would bury his face between her thighs until he'd satisfied them both. He craved her, the taste of her on his tongue.

Oh, yes, he had plans tonight. Plans that were much more

pleasurable than any he'd ever made before taking Leah as his wife.

"Uh, yeah, sure. If you don't want anything."

He lifted a shoulder, not sure why he didn't want to tell her about the candy in his pocket. "No. I don't need anything."

"Oh. Okay."

Not touching, they stepped out of the store and onto the sidewalk. And flashbulbs exploded in front of them. He was blinded by the harsh light, bright spots in the dark that marred his vision so it was all he saw everywhere he turned. He tried to look at Leah, to see her expression, but her face was obscured by spots dancing before his eyes.

"Where have you been for the past week?" One of the reporters shouted a question, and the others took it to mean it was a field day.

"Ajax! Ajax! How do you respond to allegations that your ex-fiancée left you for another man?"

"Ajax! Why the charade?"

"Leah! What's it like to be the backup bride?"

Ajax gripped Leah's arm and pulled her in tight to his body. "No questions," he growled, dragging her toward the car.

He'd always commanded a fair bit of interest from the media, but nothing like this, not ever. It was Rachel, of course, his association with Holt and what had happened at the wedding. But mainly Rachel. She was the darling of the press. Of the society world in general.

And she had, no doubt, been indiscreet with her lover. And now suddenly, he and Leah were much more fascinating than they'd been when they'd simply made up the story about the amicable split of him and Rachel, and his discovery of feelings for Leah.

As he ushered Leah into the limo, he heard one last question rise up over the others. "How does it feel to have the swan get away while you get left with the ugly duckling?"

He slammed the door shut and shouted at his driver in Greek

to drive. And then remembered his driver didn't speak Greek. The man seemed to get the gist of it, though, even if he didn't understand the exact words.

And in that spirit, Ajax let loose a string of profanity he doubted even Leah was familiar with.

His vision started to clear, slowly, and he could see Leah's face, revealed by strips of light as the car passed buildings, still open, even though it was late. Each bar of light illuminated a glittering tear on her cheek. She didn't make a sound, her face didn't crumble, she sat, stoic, with moisture tracking down her face.

The car pulled up to his penthouse, and Leah was out before the vehicle had stopped all the way. Ajax followed.

"Leah," he said.

"Don't," she said, walking on ahead of him, stopping when at the doors, waiting until he entered the building code, and then charging ahead of him again.

"What they said…"

"Was true. I am your backup, and we both know it. But it was my choice. I knew what I was getting into. But that doesn't mean I have to like hearing crap like that shouted at me in public."

"Damn right," he growled, following her into a waiting elevator. "I won't allow it to run, Leah. I won't allow a headline like that to exist."

"Control the press now, do you, darling?" she said, her tone brittle. "You're more powerful than the president."

"I have connections. And that," he spat, "isn't news. It's the lowest form of entertainment, given to people who have nothing better to do than to sit and enjoy the misery of others. The modern-day Greek tragedy."

"Yep. All the catharsis of Oedipus Rex without the incest," she bit out. "I'm so thrilled to be a part of it."

"I would have spared you from this."

"It doesn't matter, Ajax," she said, wiping a tear from her

cheek. "If they didn't print it, it wouldn't make it any less true. You wanted her...you got stuck with me."

"I didn't love her."

"But you wanted her."

He couldn't imagine taking Rachel to his bed, not even in the vaguest fantasy. He couldn't imagine having or wanting any woman other than Leah. He could picture her even now, her dark curls spread over his pillow, her arms raised above her head, pushing her breasts up. An offering. One he would always accept.

"I don't want her now." He didn't think he ever had really.

"I... That's good. But still... Backup Bride. Yay. That's catchy. That's going to stick."

"I will..."

"You will what, Ajax? Go in and be all mean and scary and demand retractions? Why? What's the point?"

He reached down and cupped her chin. "Because I will not have them hurt you like this."

"Why not? You hurt me all the time."

He dropped his hand down to his side, a strange, cold feeling spreading from his chest down to his fingertips.

The elevator doors slid open, and she walked out into the hall, standing by the door, waiting for him to open it. She pushed past him and into the living room. "So, great, I'm going to bed. And I think I'm going to let you off the hook tonight."

"Let me off the...?"

"Of our deal. Every night. My bed. I don't want to do that tonight."

"Why?" he asked, knowing it was a stupid question, and yet he had no idea how to fix the situation he found himself in. Leah had been different in the candy store. Softer for a moment. More like the Leah he'd always known.

But now her guard was up, walls strong and high around her. He couldn't reach her. Didn't know what to say or do.

"I have a headache," she said. "Something to do with over-exposure to flashbulbs. Good night."

She stalked out of the room, and Ajax walked to the bar. He kept a bar in his house, and it was fully stocked. He told himself it was for guests, but deep down he knew. He knew he was waving a red flag in front of the beast, tempting him.

And tonight…tonight he nearly took the bait.

He gritted his teeth and turned away from it. He was in control. No one would take that from him, not even Leah.

CHAPTER TWELVE

LEAH WOKE UP feeling horrible, and her mood lasted the whole day. Last night's encounter with the press had been the embodiment of her every past insecurity. Of her every current insecurity. So many people so certain she wasn't good enough. So confident in saying it. In reminding her that her husband, the man she made love with every night, didn't really want her.

She had ample time to get grouchier since Ajax spent the whole day at Holt and she spent the whole day replaying the press fiasco, and every lame encounter she and Ajax had had since their marriage, without the memory of recent good sex as a buffer.

She was digging through his freezer, looking for something for dinner, when he came back home.

"Leah," he said, coming into the room, "I hope you didn't eat."

"That was actually why I was spelunking through your freezer. I'm hungry."

"I don't have much of anything in this house. I'm not here often enough."

"Yeah, I noticed. Order a pizza?"

"No, I thought we might go out."

"Why?"

He held a newspaper out in front of him, folded open to the society pages. There was a photo, a huge photo, of her and Ajax, walking out of Leah's Lollies last night. They both looked strained, and they had a gap between their hands that looked extremely…significant. She imagined the facial expressions were from the camera. As for the not touching…well, she wasn't allowed to touch him. Not when he didn't want. So that was his fault.

The headline was *really* nice.

"Strain for Ajax Kouros and his Backup Bride as Holt Heiress Cavorts with Her New Lover. Gee. Charming." She sucked in a sharp breath and blinked against the sudden stinging in her eyes. "I'm actually a Holt heiress, too. She's not more of a Holt heiress than me. But I'm usually the Other Holt Heiress. And now I've been demoted further than even this. It's like I don't have a name. This backup bride title is bull—"

"And it's why we're going out," he said. "A show of togetherness is essential right now. I am not allowing this marriage to become a farce."

"This marriage is a farce, Ajax."

He grabbed her arm and pulled her up against him, his dark eyes blazing. "Is it? We seem to have some very real moments."

"In bed. And even then…it's a game."

"Nothing is funny about any of it, Leah. Nothing."

"I didn't say it was. But you aren't real. It's not real. You have rules, and you're like a naked referee. I can't do anything you don't want me to do."

"It's for your own good," he bit out.

"Really? And since when did you become an expert on my own good, Ajax, huh?"

"It's not you I need to know—it's me."

"And why is that?"

"Do you want to know why I haven't been with a woman in eighteen years? Do you want to know why I have to control myself. Why I have to tie your hands?"

"Yes," she said, not sure she did. Suddenly wishing she could stop the train, but it was too late. There was too much momentum.

"The night of my sixteenth birthday I nearly raped a woman."

Leah went cold. Starting at her lips, spreading through her face, down to her fingertips. The moment, and it could only have been a moment, stretched on and on. Forever.

"You…what? I don't believe you. I don't… Ajax, you didn't…"

"I did. My father never paid much attention to me. I never knew who my mother was, probably a whore, and I mean that in the literal sense. I grew up neglected, surrounded by excess. The night of my birthday, my father actually gave me a party. And drugs. A lot of drugs. Not the first time I'd ever taken them. I was, for lack of a better term, a kid in a candy store after all. But at that age, my father decided it was time for me to truly understand the products he sold, so that when I became a man I could take over the business. When I became a man like him. Not if. When."

"What…what…?"

"I was high out of my mind, I'd never had so much. And there was a party. It was so damn loud and hot. People screwing in every room in the house. In the hall. Women who were paid to be there, paid to service men, doing their jobs right there in public because they had no other choice. And then there was Celia. I know her name. I still remember it. My father shut me in a room with her, and I was…I was so certain in my own appeal, my own importance. After all, no woman had ever said no to me. Who would dare say no to the boss's son? She'd been given to me. And I wanted her. I saw nothing else but what I wanted. And hell, she'd been paid to be with me. She was my whore, right? So I was ready to just take her. And I very nearly did."

He could remember tearing her dress. Her sharp sob, fists hitting him. And everything suddenly becoming clear. Realizing what he was doing. Realizing for the first time that his pursuit of self-satisfaction had a cost for those he used.

Realizing for the very first time that other people mattered.

It was not what he had been taught. He'd been taught nothing. He'd been fighting for survival within the walls of his father's mansion. A mansion that was more of a compound. Taking what he needed, what he wanted with no consequences.

Except on one girl's tear-streaked face he suddenly saw every consequence. The weighty price of his brand of enjoying life.

"Ajax...you didn't, though. That's what matters."

"No, Leah, it's not. It's not. I...grabbed her arm and then I looked at her. I really looked. She was terrified. Crying. Because of me. Because of what I had been about to do to her. Because of what I was too blinded by myself to see."

"And the drugs. You were on drugs."

"That makes it better, Leah? I shouldn't have ever agreed to that. Much less agreed to sleep with a woman who was paid to be there. Do you know what my father said?"

She didn't want to know. "What?"

"Break her in. She's a virgin. You'll like her."

"Oh," Leah breathed, the one syllable filled with pain. For him. For Celia.

"She was just a girl. Sixteen like me, I found out later."

"How did you find out?"

"Because the minute I sobered up enough to do anything but lie on the bed and cry with her over what was happening in me, about what I'd nearly done, about what my father did, we ran. I took her back home. She wasn't a prostitute. She wasn't there because she wanted to be, or even there to get drugs. She'd been kidnapped. I couldn't go to the police. Because I knew well that many of them were on my father's payroll. How else does a man with such a transparent operation last so long? And for that betrayal...for that betrayal he would have killed me. He very possibly would have tracked down Celia's family and had her killed, too."

"Ajax that's…terrible. You had no help…no way to get out."

"She wouldn't have needed help if not for my father. If not for me."

"And you saved her." ·

"Do not turn me into the hero of this twisted story. There was nothing heroic about what I did. It was the absolute least that a human should do for another human. I will never…I will never be that man again. That man who felt like everything was for him. That man who threw off all control, who threw away everything good in him in pursuit of pleasure."

"Pleasure you didn't take."

"Stop trying to spin it so I come out looking good," he said. "A murderer might stop his knife just before it hits his victim. He might stop. But he is still, in his heart, a murderer."

"And you think you would hurt me if I pushed you too far?"

He took a deep breath, and looked at her, his black eyes blank, bottomless. "That's the thing. I have no idea what I would do. I have kept myself, so much of myself, chained for so long. All I know is that the beast is hungry. I don't know what it wants. And I damn sure will not find out at your expense."

"And this is why you were never with a woman?"

"Sex, in my mind, has a place. It is not the halls of a mansion where everyone can see. It's not with a frightened girl kidnapped from her home. Sex like that? It has a victim, Leah. I thought in marriage that dynamic would be erased." His skin turned ashen, his expression like stone. "I haven't made a victim of you, have I?"

She tilted her chin, trying to look confident, trying not to look as if she was breaking inside. Breaking for him. For all he'd been through. For how he saw himself. Ajax believed he had a beast in him. More than that, Leah thought he probably believed he was the beast.

"Ajax, I asked you to sleep with me. I told you I wanted sex. You have never done anything I haven't wanted you to. You tie my hands because I let you. I only submit because I want to. I'm strong enough to handle you."

"But I fear I'm strong enough to break you."

She shook her head. "I don't think so. Ajax…the man you are today, the man you are now…could you possibly be that man without that moment with Celia?"

"I don't understand."

"Without that moment of clarity, that moment where you first saw who you were, would you have ever changed?"

"I don't… Leah, I can't…"

"What is your father doing now?"

"He's in jail," Ajax said. "Because I used my connections to find a way to put him in there. I hope he's dead, Leah. I pray it's so."

"You put him behind bars?"

"Yes."

"And the women?"

"As far as I know, with access to all of his computers, they rescued a record number of people."

"Because of you. Because that's who you are."

"No. I'm not."

"Do you have to punish yourself?"

"I'm not punishing myself. I'm keeping those around me safe. Except you." He met her eyes, a knot forming in his chest. "I fear I'm not keeping you safe."

"Trust that I'm strong enough to keep myself safe. And to know what I want."

"And what do you want?"

"Dolmades. Take me someplace Greek."

Ajax's heart was about to wear a hole through his chest. He was still high on adrenaline after his confession to Leah. Dinner hadn't done anything to take the edge off. He wondered if he even deserved to have the edge taken off.

Because the truth was ugly. So ugly. And he deserved to burn for it.

The restaurant was small, a trendy, darkly lit place where people who were truly famous went. It was where people went who didn't want privacy. The perfect place to go to encounter the press. To have pictures taken.

The press. He had to think of the press now and not just his past. Not about the monster prowling around inside of him.

"Do you want to dance?" There was a small dance floor, near the stage. It was intimate and crowded. Just the sort of thing a newlywed couple would be drawn to. He supposed.

"I didn't think you danced."

"I don't," he said. "Now, would you like the dance or not?"

Leah cocked her head to the side, her curls spilling over her shoulder like a dark waterfall, her eyebrows locked together. "Yes. Yes, I'll dance with you."

"All right." He stood and offered her his hand. "Try not to look like I've asked you to join me in front of the firing squad, okay?"

She smiled then. "Aw, Ajax, are you trying humor?"

"Yes. Have I succeeded?"

"Almost." She took his hand. He curled his fingers around it, relishing her softness. Her warmth.

He took her down to where the other couples were, moving in time with the music and pulled her against him. Before he realized that he truly had no idea how to dance.

"I've never done this before," he said.

She laced her fingers through his, one hand on his shoulder. "That can't be. You've been to hundreds of events with Rachel."

"And I always told her what I told you that day after our wedding. I don't dance."

"So why are you dancing now?"

"Because you're right. I can't go storming into the newsroom and threaten to kill people. It wouldn't be appropriate."

"Not even a little."

"And I can't stop them from printing things like they did today. But dammit, I can work to kill the rumors. I can do my part to make sure no one, anywhere, ever assumes that you're a backup for anything."

She blinked and rested her head against his shoulder. "I am, though."

"I didn't know Rachel," he said. "Not really. We never once had a deep conversation. I never told her about my life at my father's compound. And she wouldn't have wanted to hear it. She was content to just have a facade, and that was fine by me. Preferable even. But I didn't know her. She didn't know me. I didn't know you, either. But I'm starting to. And I think…I think you now know me better than any other person on earth."

"Really?" Her words were muffled by his suit jacket.

"Yes. Really. Starting from when you used to come and visit me. Do you remember that?"

She laughed, a watery sound. "Of course."

"You brought me chocolate. It always made me… I felt like someone was thinking of me. Me, not my business acumen, or anything else. Just me. And now you're the only woman who knows about my past. The only woman who has ever been with me…as a man. As anything other than the stupid, selfish boy I was. So I think you officially know me better than anyone."

"I guess I do."

"And you're here with me. You didn't run. And now that I know you, now that I know you as a woman, a woman who will not hesitate to yell at me, to take a cut out of my ego with a sassy remark, I find that…I find that I don't believe another woman would be right for me."

"But am I right for you? Or is it just that anyone would be wrong?" She lifted her head and looked at him, golden eyes sparkling.

"I don't know. But we're together."

"After three weeks of marriage. Someone get us a medal."

"I don't know that I really understand love… I doubt I ever will. I thought I did, but it's become very clear that I knew an attachment for convenience, and not any sort of real affection or deep emotion. I don't know if I'm wired to…to know how to give it. My father didn't love anything but money and power. He taught me to view myself as the final authority, be my own god, worship myself and my needs and…that one moment in my life, when I saw her face…" It made his chest tight to think about it, even after all these years. "That was the first time I ever looked outside of myself. The first time I considered that other people had feelings and needs and hopes and dreams that were just as important as mine. More important. And that I possessed the power to destroy them if I had a mind to."

Her fingers curled around his suit jacket, her hold on him tight. He continued. "Just that bit of humanity was a lot of effort to achieve and beyond that…I try to keep my needs, my desires, under control so that I at least don't hurt anyone. I can't be everything a husband should be, but I won't be cruel. I won't ever hurt you or force you, or do anything that you don't want me to."

Leah's heart thundered, her hands shaking. She was holding on to Ajax as tightly as she could to keep from crumpling to the floor.

He was telling her about himself. Everything he believed about himself. And he was, in the same breath, promising never to hurt her. And his words were destroying every wall she'd built between them.

Didn't he know? Didn't he have any idea that marriage to a man who kept half of his heart, half of who he was, prisoner deep down inside himself would be able to do nothing but hurt her? Even if the hurt only came from watching him. Day after day, struggling with what he considered to be an inner demon, when it was simply Ajax. He fought against himself, waged a war on appetites most people embraced. The appetites most people found made life worth living.

Didn't he know that it would kill her to watch it?

She looked at him, at the horrible blankness in his eyes, and she pictured his fire, his life, pushed down deep in his body, crying our for release. For freedom.

She had spent her life idolizing Ajax Kouros. A man who she thought had it all. A man she thought to be perfect. But she hadn't known Ajax. Hadn't known the struggles he'd faced, where he'd come from, or why he was headed toward his final destination with such singular purpose.

She hadn't known how hard his fight was. Hadn't known that every day cost him more energy just to keep himself in line than most people would ever have to expend.

She had loved an illusion. And now before her was the man. Or part of him anyway. She wanted the rest. She wanted all of him. She wanted to know him. To know the things about him even he didn't know, the things he wouldn't acknowledge.

And she realized something suddenly. That she was selling them both short. Yes, she'd purposed not to protect herself quite so much. To view him with realism. To accept he couldn't love her. That he couldn't love.

And in turn, she wouldn't love him. She wouldn't be vulnerable to him. She wouldn't give what she couldn't get.

She was taking half willingly. Pushing him for nothing, because if she pushed him for emotion, for love, she would have to acknowledge that she wanted it. That she wanted more than sex and companionship.

She would expose herself to the kind of pain the media had never come close to doling out.

She had just thought of him as a man denying himself, but was she any better? She was protecting herself. Protecting herself by denying a piece of her that was bound up, gasping for breath.

The part of herself who believed she deserved to try for it

all, pain be damned. Who believed her happiness was worth risking her heart. Who believed Ajax's happiness was worth risking her heart.

"So…" She swallowed. "What you're saying is, if you could go back to the moment you proposed, knowing what you know now…you would ask me instead?"

He nodded slowly, still swaying, almost in time with the music. "Yes."

She sucked in a sharp breath. "I…I'm not sure I·would say yes."

His brows locked together. "Why?"

It was time to let her guard down. Really. It was time to have expectations. To believe she could make him change. To believe she wasn't the Backup Bride.

"You give this big talk about knowing me, Ajax, but I don't feel like I know you. I can't even explore your body when we're in bed together. Which means…you don't really know me, either. You have me on a leash. Following your rules so you can hang on to that control you love so much."

"I don't mean to leash you, Leah. It's myself that I—"

"That might be what you mean to be doing, but the fact is, when you impose rules like that, stop me from doing what I want, from showing you what I want, you're only making me the person you expect me to be, the person you think you need me to be. Rather than the person I am. No wonder it's been so good for you. But you could have what you have with me with any other woman. Any obedient woman, that is."

He spun her out from his body, then pulled her back in, dipping his face close to hers.

"Not bad," she said.

"Thank you, I learn fast."

"Yes, you do."

"So you think I don't allow you to be who you are? Have I stopped you from saying…any and everything that comes to your mind? You, daily, take strips off me with your tongue, my dear, and I've hardly done anything about that, now, have I?"

Yes, she'd done that. Often. Self-protection. An attempt to push him away. To derail him. But she wasn't doing that now.

She gritted her teeth and pulled her fingers from his, took her hand from his shoulders and cupped his face. He stopped moving, his expression confused. She found it endearing. That big strong Ajax Kouros was confused by little ol' her.

"I'm sorry," she said. "I do that because sometimes when you hurt my feelings it's easier to yell at you than it is to show you that I'm hurt. And tonight, Ajax, just tonight, mind you—I can't put a moratorium on the sarcasm forever—I'm going to stop. But I need something in return."

"What?"

"I need you to play by my rules. Just for tonight."

"After everything I told you about me?" he asked, his voice rough.

"If you lose control are you going to hurt me?"

He looked scared. Haunted. "I don't know."

"I do. You won't. That isn't what you are. Men who delight in hurting women…it's not about desire. Or losing control because they're around a woman they can't resist. Those are lies. Those men want to hurt. They want to make themselves powerful. I have never seen those desires in you."

"Leah…"

"My rules, okay, not yours. Tonight. Come on, you're already dancing. It's nothing but a little quickstep to hell after this. We might as well have some fun on the way."

"What are your rules?" he asked. His face was like stone, immobile, unreadable.

She leaned in, her lips touching his ear. "I was thinking, my hands, untied. And I get to do whatever I want to you. And Ajax, my darling, I have about ten years' worth of fantasies stored up for you."

"Ten years?"

"All right, we'll skip the early years. That was a lot of running through meadows and you braiding flowers in my hair. But things started getting good about the time I was sixteen."

"Fantasies? About me?"

She smiled. "You didn't think I left candy on your desk just to be nice, did you?"

"I did, yes. It meant a lot to me, as I said. Are you telling me you were baiting me?"

"A little candy trail that I hoped might lead you to my bed."

"Subtle," he said. "Too subtle."

"I realize that now."

He frowned. "Why me?"

"Because I thought you were perfect. And gorgeous. I was wrong."

His frown deepened. "Were you?"

"Not about the gorgeous part, about the perfect part. I made you something in my head that I shouldn't have. You aren't perfect, Ajax. But the thing is, I'm not a girl anymore. And I don't need you to be perfect."

"What do you need?" he asked, an edge of desperation to his voice.

"I just need you. The man you are. The man you have become because of your mistakes. Because of your scars. Not the man you are with all those chains on, but the man you *are*."

"You say that, Leah, but you don't know."

"You told me."

"I told you who I saw myself becoming, and why, but I don't even know what would happen now…I don't even know if I could change the way I do things, the way I see things. And I doubt you would like me if I did."

"Here's the thing—I don't know if I would, either. But you have to give me a chance to know you. Give yourself the chance to be you. And I'll give you a chance to know me."

He lifted his hand, cupped her cheek, then slid his fingers

through her hair, letting the strands fall around her face. "But there is every chance that once you know me, you won't like me."

She took his hand and turned his palm toward her face, pressing a kiss to his skin. "Ajax, you danced for me. So that the press wouldn't say horrible things about me. I like what I know of you. A lot."

"Even knowing my past?"

"Your past breaks my heart. I can't imagine what it must have been like to be a child in a place like that. To have a father like that."

"What if…what if you dig so deep, Leah, deep inside of me, and you find out the darkness just keeps going? That there's no end to it. What if this is all I am?"

She blinked back the tears that were stinging her eyes. And she didn't try that hard to hold them back. Her heart ached, her throat burning.

Because she didn't know the answer to that question. If her husband could only ever give her this, what would it mean? If, after deciding to give it all, she could only get crumbs in return, what would she do?

It made her want to fold in on herself and start building new armor. To push him away. To retreat into a place where she was safe. From comparisons made by him, made by the media. From the deep fear that one day she would look into his eyes, searching for the truth of his feelings, and see nothing. From anything that might hurt her.

But she couldn't do that. Not now. Never again.

"Then I will take everything you are," she said, the words heavy on her tongue. The vow heavy in her heart, on her shoulders. Because in that moment she knew it was true. And she knew she couldn't go back on it.

But as she looked into his dark, fathomless eyes she wished she could. She wished some other man had claimed her heart years ago so that she wasn't so vulnerable to this one.

But there was no other man. There was only Ajax. It had always been that way, and she knew, beyond a shadow of a doubt, that it always would be.

Every muscle in Ajax's body was locked tight, ready to release at any moment. To pounce on Leah, maybe? Or to run. That was the other possibility.

They'd driven back to the penthouse in total silence, Leah wringing her hands in the seat next to him, looking out the window and most definitely not at him. And he wondered if she was already regretting what she'd asked of him.

He was at war. He wanted her. Wanted her hands all over his body, her mouth on him. But he knew that if that happened, in one blinding moment years of hard-won control could be undone, and he might never get it back.

That he could become the monster he had always feared he was.

The beast he kept chained inside of him, was him. He knew it, had always known it. And it terrified him down to his soul. That if he ever let it go, those parts of himself would meld back together, and there would be no more separating it.

That he would become the thing he hated most. Oh, he didn't think he would become a drug lord. But a man consumed by the desire for power? For success? At the expense of all else?

Yes, that lived in him. That horrible, conscienceless drive lived in him. Strong and black, seeking to devour whatever it could on the path to success. Not just success, to ultimate, unquestionable power, and damn who was hurt in the process.

He didn't want that to have free rein. Ever.

But now he was standing in the bedroom at his penthouse, and Leah was looking at him with wide golden eyes, fringed with dark lashes. Her lips were painted red, her dress, a deep green, molded to her curves, and he stood ready to trade everything in for the chance to taste her with no limits.

To have her with no ties to hold her back.

Yes, that was what he wanted. So badly he ached with it. And he didn't have the power to fight it anymore. Suddenly, having her seemed to be the most essential thing he could imagine. The embodiment of a dream, buried so deep, for so long, that unearthing it was nearly painful.

"Show me, Leah," he said. "Show me what you want. Show me who you are."

CHAPTER THIRTEEN

"You first." She tilted her chin up, her hip cocked to the side, her eyes glittering. "I feel like I've been doing a lot of giving here lately. Not that you don't…give admirably during our encounters—you do. But I feel like I'm the vulnerable one, so now it's your turn. Get naked, Ajax."

Her command felt like it was for more than skin. Like she wanted the kind of nakedness he was most afraid of. The kind that would reveal more than his body. The kind that would reveal what was left of his soul, and the state it was in.

But for her he would.

He started unbuttoning his shirt, then his pants, and he stood before her, naked. Shaking. She was unbound; she could do with him what she wanted. He was at her mercy, and he didn't regret it.

She approached slowly, a low flame burning in her eyes, gold flickering in the dim light. She reached out and put her hand on his bare chest, nails raking over his flesh, lightly. The slight pain was, as it had been their first time, a welcome gift to help temper the pleasure that was holding him by the throat.

And then she kissed him there, her lips hot on his neck, her teeth grazing him slightly. A testament of her power. That she held him in thrall using no force, only touch.

The beast rattled the chains.

"Careful," he said, his voice rough.

She bit him harder, scoring sensitive flesh. "I don't think I will be. I'm tired of being careful. I'm tired of holding back. I'm tired of being…I'm tired of trying to seem unaffected by the crap that gets written about me in newspapers. I'm tired of trying to keep my head down so I can avoid it. I'm tired of trying to make myself more attractive or more palatable to the public. I'm tired of hiding myself. Of changing myself to suit people who will always find me wanting no matter what I do. But most of all, I'm tired of not having my way with you."

"Then take me. But I can't be responsible for the consequences."

"Oh, I hope there are consequences," she said. "Don't make promises you can't keep."

He grabbed her wrists and pulled her forward, bringing her breasts up hard against his chest, his erection pressing against her belly. "There will be, *agape*. Make no mistake." He lowered his head and claimed her lips, sliding his tongue between them, delving deep.

When they parted, they were both breathing hard, Leah's face flushed, her eyes bright. She looked down at him, aching for release, her admiration open, her desire obvious.

"Right now, you're about to face some consequences of your own," she said. "I feel like I've been on a diet for years. And I am starving now."

She leaned in and kissed his chest, kissed a trail down his abs, lingering at his hip bone, biting him gently there, making him jump. She wrapped her fingers around his shaft, squeezing him gently, and he jerked beneath her hand.

"Are these my consequences?" he asked, his throat constricted.

"I'm just getting started. I have really, really fantasized about this. You have no idea." She leaned in and touched her tongue to the tip of his length, and a shot of heat scorched along his veins. Too much. It was too much.

He could feel something breaking loose inside of him. Could feel the walls starting to crumble. Chains starting to break.

When she slid her tongue along his length, he nearly lost his grip. On his control. On everything.

He pulled away from her, his heart pounding, his breath ragged. "I can't... Leah, stop."

"Why?" she asked, sounding dazed.

"It's too much. I can't...I can't breathe."

"Now you know how I feel. All the time. Every time I'm with you. Let me." She leaned in and pressed her lips to his hardened length, then her tongue. Then she sucked him deep inside of her mouth, and he was plunged into darkness, a world of absolute pleasure. Of nothing beyond what she made him feel. It roared through him, consuming him.

He clung to her, his fingers buried in her hair as she licked and sucked him, poured out her desire to give him pleasure. It humbled him. Sent him to the edge of reason, of thought.

And when he felt his climax surging through him, he pulled back.

"Not like that," he said.

"Why not?" she asked. "You've done it like that for me plenty of times."

"I know. But I want to be in you," he said, watching her face as he told her in blunt, descriptive terms, just what he wanted from her. "I want you to ride me." One position they hadn't been able to accomplish with her hands bound.

She smiled, a vixen's smile. Leah was pure seductress. A woman. And he felt for her what a man should feel for a woman. But beneath that was a warmth he couldn't explain. One that had always been there, one that had built and built from the moment he'd first met her. When she'd left candy on his desk.

The reason he'd turned his focus somewhere else as soon as possible. The reason he had never, ever seen her as a woman before the wedding.

Emotion. Passion.

That warmth, added to the desire, made a fire so hot he thought it might consume them both.

And then he remembered the candy.

"Lie down on the bed," he said.

"I thought I was giving orders."

"No. We just got rid of the rules."

"What are you planning?"

"You just have to find out. But you won't, if you don't obey."

"My consequences?"

"You could say that."

She got onto the bed, and heard rustling behind him as he turned to get the bag of candy out of his jacket pocket, where he'd left it the night before.

When he turned, she was lying on her back, her elbows propping her up. She'd discarded her shoes, her dress, her underwear. Everything. And she looked like a fantasy, created and come to life just for him. Nothing could have been more perfect; no one else could have even come close.

"You're a step ahead of me."

"I take initiative," she said. "It's one of my better qualities."

He approached the bed, the bag in his hand.

"Why do you have a Leah's Lollies bag?" she asked, eyes narrowed.

"I bought these a few nights ago. I wasn't sure why then. But I am now." He opened the bag and reached in, pulling out one red, round candy and placing it on her thigh. He leaned in, pressed his lips to her, then took the candy between his teeth. Then he licked her skin clean, the cherry flavor mingling with the taste of her. "Lie down."

He didn't have to ask her twice. Her hands were at her sides, her breasts rising and falling rapidly with each breath. He placed one candy just below her belly button, then another next to it, and another. Until he made a crimson, winding trail over her stomach, to her breasts, three pieces going just between them.

Then he placed one on her lips.

"Hold it there," he said.

She nodded slightly.

And he looked down at the trail of temptation on her beautiful body. "I always thought you were sweet," he said.

He lowered his head and flicked his tongue over her clitoris, and she bucked beneath him, a short, muffled sound escaping her lips. "Careful," he said. "Don't lose my reward."

He moved to the candy that rested low on her stomach, just above the triangle of curls at the apex of her thighs, taking it with his teeth as he'd done with the first, then lapping at her skin, taking in the flavor of cherry and Leah.

Ajax followed the trail, to her breasts, pausing to trace her nipples with the tip of his tongue before sucking them deep, savoring them as he'd done the candy. No extra adornment was needed there, not at all. They were delicious enough without adding any sugar.

He moved to the valley between her breasts and lapped up the remaining treats before moving to her mouth, his lips hovering over hers. He traced the seam of her lips with his tongue and captured the candy before kissing her deeply.

"You taste like cherry," she said at last, her voice breathy.

"So do you."

She laughed. "Funny how that works."

He gripped her hips and flipped their position so that she was sitting on top of him, straddling him, her hair forming a silken curtain around them, his cock resting against the slick entrance to her body.

She put her hands on his shoulders, moved herself into position, taking him in, inch by inch. And he watched her face, watched the expression of pure pleasure as it took her over. And then he was too far gone to do anything but feel.

He was at her mercy, her tight, wet heat surrounding him, her rhythm, slow and steady, driving him to madness. And suddenly he felt desperate. Desperate and starving, a gaping pit opening up inside of him, of need, of desire, that he feared could never be satisfied.

He reversed positions again and closed his eyes, pounding into her, the sheets fisted into his hands, sweat breaking out over his skin. And blood roaring through his veins. The beast unleashed. His need so overpowering, so violent and intense that Ajax lost control completely, his entire being one with the hunger, with the drive to claim her, make her his, find the ultimate pleasure with her. In her.

His woman. His wife. Leah.

A hoarse cry escaped her lips, her back arching, internal muscles pulsing around him. And he let go, spilling himself inside of her, his orgasm a flame, weaving itself through every fiber of his body, burning him from the inside out, the white wash of heat so intense he thought there would be nothing left of him when it was all over.

And finally it passed. And there was nothing left but him, and Leah. And the realization that all of his walls were gone. That he was torn open. Bloody. Defenseless. He had unleashed the beast on Leah.

He pulled away from her, scrambled into a standing position, his heart pounding hard, his breath coming in harsh gasps. He looked at Leah, at her swollen lips, her round eyes, filled with shock, confusion.

And he turned and walked out of the room.

Leah was stunned. Devastated, really. Her world was completely shaken by her encounter with Ajax. There wasn't cold darkness down deep in him. He was full of black fire, hot and dangerous, destructive and amazing.

She would never get enough of him, of how it felt to have all of his passion unleashed on her. The way it had started, the way he'd responded to her tasting him, the sexy playfulness of the candy. And then…oh, and then. That moment when he'd lost all control and put every ounce of his power into pleasuring them both. That moment when he'd unleashed himself on her.

She felt raw. Sore in the absolute best way. She liked him when he was rough. When he was uncivilized. When he was the man beneath the veneer.

What she didn't like was him walking away while her world was shattered around her feet.

She stood up and put his shirt on, buttoning it as quickly as she could, on her way out to the living room.

"Hey," she said. "What the hell? Unless you're just getting a glass of water, in which case I'll have one, too."

Ajax was pacing up and down the floor like a caged tiger, his posture tense. And he was still completely naked. He was beautiful, even like this. Tense and upset, and clearly on the edge.

"What's up, Ajax? Walk me through your thought process here. Because we were making love and doing this whole 'get to know each other' thing and then you…left."

"Are you okay?" he asked, his voice rough.

"Fine. A little wobbly, but I think you should be after something like that. Means you did it right."

"Stop. Stop trying to make a joke out of everything," he said, the words torn from him. "I was rough with you. I don't even know… I can't even remember what I did."

"Let me refresh your memory." She walked down to the center of the room. "You lost control. You thrust into me so hard it took my breath away. And it gave me pleasure that went… way beyond anything I've ever experienced before."

"Did I hurt you?"

"No. Well, I mean I'm sore in places, but the good kind."

"There's no good kind of pain. Dammit, Leah, if you had told me to stop I might not even have heard you. I don't know if I could have stopped. That's the kind of monster I am."

His words hung in the air, stark and revealing.

"You didn't hurt me, Ajax, and you never would. It's…it's

just…don't you trust that I know what I want? That I know what I like? That I would never in a million years lie to you if you hurt me just to salve your conscience? You know me. You know I would never do that to you, to *us*. I have been honest with you," she said, and then bitterly regretted saying it.

Because she hadn't been honest with him. She hadn't even been honest with herself. She'd pushed at him, had tried to cover up the growing, expanding emotions inside of her with layers of protection.

So that she wouldn't fall in love.

So that she wouldn't have to be in love alone.

She'd walked into her marriage with an impression she had of Ajax based in fantasy, not in reality. Thinking that she was in no way susceptible to this man. The man she hadn't known.

And since then, she'd met the reality. She'd seen how far down his damage had gone. She'd had to face who he was, where he came from. That he wasn't a shining beacon of male perfection, but a damaged, wounded soul who was starving for love, for affection, and to find some kind of peace within himself.

Because the inside of Ajax was a war zone. A place without rest. A place where he stood vigil against any desire he possessed. She doubted he even let go in his own mind. He was enslaved, in bondage.

He had tied her hands at first when they'd made love, but he was really the one that was bound.

And faced with that, with all he was, all he had been, and all he might not be, she knew her feelings had changed.

And she couldn't keep them in anymore. Not now, not after everything they'd shared. She couldn't protect herself when the victory over his demons might depend on her honesty.

"I love you," she said. It was true now. Truer than it had ever been. And the risk didn't matter. The possibility of him never returning it didn't matter. It would hurt, but sharing it was so much more important than protecting herself.

In Ajax, she'd seen the danger of holding it all in, and she wouldn't do it. Not anymore. Not ever again. It didn't matter that the press didn't think she was the pretty Holt Heiress, or that it must suck for Ajax to have her instead of Rachel.

It didn't matter. All that mattered was how she felt. That she loved him.

"What?" He looked at her with black, blank eyes, and the lack of emotion in them nearly broke her then and there.

"I love you," she said. "I have…well, I've loved you, or at least I thought I did, for most of my life. And there was a time when…when I tried to dig it out of my chest. To make it go away. Because I needed to protect myself. Because you chose her. Because the press told me who I was. That I wasn't special or pretty, and I thought… I was sure I couldn't ever be enough for you. But you know what? I could keep it inside then because I didn't *really* love you."

"I would think not," he said, his voice hard.

"I didn't know you. I didn't know you'd been raised in a drug house and brothel. I didn't know you felt like you were a monster, that you kept so much of yourself in chains. I didn't know you lost your virginity to a prostitute. That you'd run from a certain position of power and wealth into nothing to save the life of a girl. To save your own soul. I didn't know you hadn't touched a woman for eighteen years for fear you might relinquish hold on your control."

"You're quite fixated on that."

"Yeah, well, I think it's kind of hot. Really hot, actually. I'm glad I was your first in so much time. I'm glad you were my first ever. And that's the thing, really, I'm glad that I know you. Even if the truth isn't easy. Even if it's not pretty. Because now that I *know* you, Ajax…everything you were, everything you are, *now* I love you."

"You just said…"

"That I didn't love you before. I loved the idea of you, but not you. Not the broken mess you are."

"You shouldn't love the mess I am. I'm…I'm…"

"You're a monster, so I've heard. A monster who has not once done anything to hurt me physically. A monster who spent all these years giving nothing but respect to my family. A monster who dismantled one of the world's most insidious crime rings. Yeah, you're a monster."

"You don't understand," he said.

And then she saw it. The terror in his eyes, the depth of fear, and she did understand.

"I do," she said. "I do understand."

"If you did, you wouldn't be standing here offering me anything but a divorce. If you really knew…"

"Ajax, you are a damn coward," she said.

"Because I want to protect you?"

"Because you want to protect *you!*" she said. "I know because until tonight, I was doing the same thing. This is the honest truth of it, Ajax. You aren't afraid of what will get out. You're afraid of what will get in. I know your life was hard. I know it was…more than I can possibly imagine. I know that. And I know that you had to go down deep to forget, to protect yourself."

He closed the distance between her and grabbed her arms. "You think I'm afraid? That I'm some sort of victim? Was I the one huddled on a bed crying while some asshole who was high out of his mind tried to force himself on me? No. Don't try to make me out to be anything other than what I was. What I am."

"It was a terrible thing, Ajax. The whole situation. But in the end, when that woman looks back on her life, how do you think she sees you? As a monster? Or as her savior? Because if it hadn't been you in that room with her, it would have been someone else. And would they have stopped when they saw her tears? Or would they have kept on? Would they have forced themselves on her without a thought? Would they have left her there in your father's compound? Would she have ever seen her family again?"

"Stop," he said, turning away from her.

"You need this lie, don't you? That you're somehow beyond redemption, because it gives you an excuse to cut yourself off from the world and then you don't have to admit how scared you are."

"This is all there is, Leah. This isn't a lie. This is just me. You can't possibly love this." He hit himself in the chest with his closed fist.

"Why not?"

"Because *I* don't!" he roared. "Because I *truly* know me. And I despise everything in there. I changed my name, I left my home. But none of that changes what I am on the inside, who I am. And if you…if you can somehow see past that? You're a damn fool, Leah Holt. I will do nothing but drag you down to hell with me, so if you have a brain in your stubborn head you'll get dressed and walk out the door."

Something in her broke. Her heart probably. Because there was so much truth in what he said. He hated himself, and she saw it now, could see just how broken he was, how sharp and jagged the pieces of him were. Always cutting, always leaving scars.

"No," she said. "I'm not going to leave. I'm not going to walk away just because it's hard." She wouldn't give up. She wouldn't hide. Always she was hiding. To avoid comparison, criticism, to avoid feeling vulnerable, but that had to stop. She wouldn't do it now. Not with him.

"This is as easy as it will ever be, *agape*," he said. "This… this won't work."

"No way, Ajax." She shook her head. "No way. You are not doing this. I am your wife. I am the only woman you have ever been naked with, and I don't mean your body. Yes, there were women before me, but they didn't have your soul. I see you, and I think that's the thing that scares you the most."

"It should scare *you*."

"Yeah, it scares me a little. Not because I think you would

ever do anything to hurt me. It scares me because I want you to love me, Ajax. I want you to open yourself up and take a chance. I want you to stop protecting yourself. Do you know how much it took for me to do it? To stand here and tell you that I love you? I want to mean enough to you that you would do the same for me."

"I don't love you," he said.

"No." Her throat started to tighten, her fingers going numb, tears stinging her eyes. "Don't…don't say that."

"You want me to lie to make you feel better?"

"I want you to tell the truth." Because this couldn't be it. How could he stand there and tell her he didn't love her after what had happened in the bedroom just a few moments before? A moment that had been so perfect? So incredible?

It had been love. It *had* to be love. Because it was for her. Truly. Deeply.

"I don't love you," he bit out, every word final, painful.

"Okay." She nodded and tried to swallow, blinking back tears. "Okay." It came out choked, weak. Utterly revealing. She felt like a little vulnerable sea creature that had been dragged out of its shell. So exposed. So naked and fragile.

She wanted to push at him. Shout at him. Do anything she could to cover up the pain.

But she wouldn't hide. She wouldn't. Not now. He deserved to see it, to see what life was like when you came out from behind the walls.

A tear slid down her cheek, and she sank down onto the couch, covering her mouth with her hand. Another tear followed the first. Then another.

"Leah?"

A sob shook her frame, and she put her other hand up, covering the first, as if it might keep her from flying apart completely. She was unprotected, for the first time in years. Hideously vulnerable. Coming apart.

"Leah," he said again.

She just shook her head.

"I refuse to be manipulated," he said, his voice low, harsh. "If you think tears are going to change my mind…"

She dropped her hands, wiped her arm over her cheek. "I have more pride than that!"

"Clearly you don't."

"Am I making you uncomfortable? If you were a real boy, you would know that this is normal. You see, Ajax, this is what people do when their hearts are broken. This is how people feel when they have their love thrown back at them!" Her voice broke, her words sounding hysterical. And she didn't care. "I'm so sorry this bothers you, because it's a picnic for me."

"Maybe that's why I don't understand. Maybe that's why I don't care. I don't have a heart." He walked past her back into the bedroom, and she just sat on the couch, staring ahead at nothing. He returned a moment later dressed in a T-shirt and jeans.

"I'm leaving," he said. "Because I have a feeling you're too stubborn to do it."

"Shall I expect something from your lawyer?"

"Yes."

"The business?"

"The least of my concerns at the moment."

That was more resounding than a slap in the face. That he would walk away from everything, from the reason they had been forced to marry in the first place, now, to get away from her.

"And if I'm pregnant? Because we haven't used a single condom."

"We'll figure out custody. I'm not going to leave you help-less."

She bit the inside of her cheek, took a deep, fortifying breath. "You couldn't. I have a successful business. I have millions of dollars. I've never been helpless. The simple truth is that I've never needed you. I just *wanted* you. I just love you. But I want you a lot less right now, so maybe you should just go."

He nodded, a muscle twitching in his jaw, like there were words built up, stopped in his throat. Words he wouldn't let out.

Then he turned and walked out of the room. The slam of the door the final word on the end of the marriage.

CHAPTER FOURTEEN

IT HAD BEEN the only thing to do. Ajax was sure of that. He'd had no other choice.

I love you.

They were the three most terrifying words he could think of Leah saying. Because that meant there was an expectation to give more than he could.

He gritted his teeth. Not more than he could, more than he wanted to.

He paced the hotel room, the one he'd got after leaving the penthouse, replaying those last moments with her. Wearing his shirt, the hem barely touching the top of her thighs. Her cheeks streaked with tears, her eyes filled with the kind of pain and misery he saw in his nightmares.

It would have been so easy to lie. To keep taking from her. To preserve his relationship, not just with her but with her father, the only good influence in his life when he'd been a teenager.

He'd been faced with this in the past. That girl who looked at him with such trust. A beautiful sixteen-year-old who was, yes, round, and a little frizzy, but, he knew, had the potential to become his entire world.

He hadn't even let himself complete the thought then. Hadn't let himself admit how much she could mean to him. Instead, he'd turned his attention somewhere else. Somewhere safer. Yes, it would have been easy to keep her. Letting her go, keeping her from being hurt by the monster, that had been the hard thing. The right thing. Because he couldn't give her what she needed. He didn't have it in him. The only thing he had in him was the potential to destroy her.

Liar.

Her words rang in his ears. Scared. Coward.

She had bared herself to him, given him everything. And still he hid.

You aren't afraid of what will get out, you're afraid of what will get in.

And then he let himself remember, really remember, the night at his father's house. That last night there. The terror of the girl. His own fear. The way the drug had twisted his thoughts, the way he'd been so sick after. The horror. The stark realization of what his father did. Of what he could become. Of the fact that there was good and evil in the world, and if he didn't do something soon he would be on the side of evil.

In one night, his world had been torn to pieces. Savaged.

He'd looked outside of himself, outside of the reality he'd been presented, and he saw all the pain, all the abuse, all of the ways a person could be destroyed, corrupted and perverted and he shut it all down

Every desire. Every emotion. For fear he would have the wrong one.

For fear all of that horror, all of that pain, would get him.

He'd tried to get rid of the feeling. Had tried by taking down his father's organization, but it hadn't worked. He'd saved the damn world and he hadn't been able to save himself.

And so he'd built walls, shoved it all down deep, turned it all off. And walked away.

And then came Leah. She'd torn down the walls with her hands tied behind her back, quite literally. And he didn't like it. It burned. It felt like his skin had been stripped off. Like old wounds had been reopened, scars carved away, leaving all of his tender flesh exposed.

He stalked to the bar and pulled out a bottle of whiskey. Expensive. High quality. But that didn't matter. As long as it would take away his pain, for a moment. Just a moment.

He thought back to his wedding day, about how tempted he'd been to lose himself then, tempted to cover the disaster in a haze.

But he hadn't.

He stood for a moment, regarding the bottle. Then he took a glass out from beneath the bar and filled it.

He wouldn't find answers in the bottom of a glass of whiskey. He wouldn't find hope or salvation there. He wouldn't even find a meaningful salve for his pain.

But maybe, just maybe, he would find rock bottom. At least if he landed there, the only way would be up.

He smiled as he raised the glass to his lips.

There wasn't enough candy in the world to make her day any sweeter. And seeing those stupid cherry buttons, the kind Ajax had eaten off her skin, just made her want to cry all over again. And if not cry, throw things and sit in the corner with a bar of chocolate. Or twenty.

She hated this. She hated being away from him. She hated how badly he'd hurt her. She hated that, for one blinding moment in time she'd nearly had everything, and now it was gone.

She was an idiot. She should have shut up and kept her marriage. She should have kept sleeping with him every night and said *I love you* over and over again in her head as she fell asleep. She shouldn't have said anything to him.

No, she should have. Leah started opening boxes of candy and loading the big glass display jars in the window. As long as she was in New York she was going to spend some time in her flagship store. Working there was therapeutic. Working with candy was therapeutic. As was eating it.

Except those cherry buttons. She was getting rid of those. She looked up from filling the jars and saw that one of the big foam glitter lollies that normally stood up nice and tall in the display window was lying against the glass. She growled and dropped the candy bag, then stepped over her faux cotton candy mist that was placed around the display floor, trying to get to the lollipop.

She started losing her balance and braced herself, her palm flat on the window. She cursed under breath. Now it would need to be cleaned, and that was just extra work because she was a clumsy idiot who loved a man who just didn't love her.

Yeah, what if that was all it was. What if he wasn't lying? What if he wasn't scared? What if he just didn't love her?

She felt like she'd just been punched in the stomach. She sank down slowly, in the fake cotton candy, the big lollipop trees overhead. And she just felt sad. A tear slid down her cheek and she wiped it away.

Would there ever be a day she didn't cry over Ajax? Yes. There would be. Of course there would be. Because wounds didn't hurt like this forever. But some of them never truly went away. And this was more than a wound. This was like losing a part of herself, a part she hadn't realized she'd been missing.

A part she didn't think she'd ever be able to replace.

So no, she wouldn't always cry. But there would always be a piece missing from her heart.

She stood and exited the display, collecting her purse and coat, avoiding making eye contact with any of the store's employees or customers. She pushed open the door and went out into the chilly afternoon, tugging her jacket on as she did so.

She pulled up the collar of her coat, and as she did, a female reporter with a recorder advanced on her, along with two men, one of whom held a video camera, the other a microphone.

Every insecurity, every fear, flooded her, oozed from the soles of her shoes and kept her rooted to the spot.

"Ms. Holt, rumor is your husband checked into a hotel last night? Any comment? Is there trouble in paradise? What will you do if you lose him?"

She almost laughed. Because she *had* lost him. And then because she realized that nothing, after this, could ever hurt her again.

She raised her hand and indicated the building behind her. "I will go to work. Because I'm the owner of a very successful chain of candy shops. I'm an entrepreneur. A businesswoman. I am not simply another Holt heiress. I am not Ajax Kouros's backup bride. I have my own identity, my own success."

She was yelling now. She probably seemed completely unhinged. Years of pent-up rage at every member of the press who had ever abused her, pouring out onto this one woman. But she didn't care. She'd always thought this, but she'd never been bold enough to say it. Ajax had made her bold enough. He'd made her believe she deserved more. That she deserved better.

That she deserved, not to modify her behavior to suit other people, but to step out from behind her sister's shadow and demand respect.

"I am not defined by my family name," she continued, "or by how I compare to my sister. I am not defined by my husband. I have a name. I'm Leah Holt, and I'm second to no one. I'm simply myself."

Ajax stared at his phone from his position on the floor of his hotel room, at the hazy headline on the entertainment section of the paper.

Leah Holt Declares: I am not defined by my husband!

Good for her. He laughed and the sound sent a wave of pain through his head. Rock bottom was a real place. It was inside of him now. His chest felt torn to bloody shreds. His head felt like it was going to burst. But nothing, nothing matched the pain in his heart.

She'd been right about him. He was nothing more than a coward. He'd done nothing more than hide, than protect himself from any potential pain, any emotion, for so many years. Too many years.

Oh, those whiskey-colored eyes. He'd looked at them, even back when she'd been a teenager, and he'd known that she could destroy him. That she could have power over him, utterly. Completely. And so he had hidden.

He was still hiding. Hungover and hiding. Not anymore. No more.

He wanted to call Leah, but he didn't know what to say. He wanted to call her father, but he really didn't know what to say.

That left one number.

He dialed a number he hadn't used in a while.

"This is Rachel."

"Do you know where Leah is?" He didn't bother with a greeting.

"Yes. And if you don't, I don't think I'm in a position to tell you. Especially not given current headlines."

"I made a mistake."

"I know you broke my sister's heart. I can't forgive that, Jax."

"I don't want absolution from you," he growled. "I want my wife back."

"I had to walk away from you for my own reasons. Partly because I wouldn't simply be married to a man who saw me as a convenience. If Leah wants more than that, if she wants love, let her go. Let her have it."

"I love her," he said, his voice rough, his body shaking.

"You…you do?"

"More than anything. Please. I need to talk to her. In person. I have a lot of…groveling to do."

There was a long pause. "Okay, Jax. I'll help you."

There had always been something comforting about the Holt Estate in Rhodes. From the moment he'd first set foot on the estate as an emotionally battered boy, it had felt right. Now, when Ajax walked up to the door, he realized what it was. It felt like home. It felt like home in a way nothing else ever had.

Strange that he could connect it now. And it seemed obvious, too.

As did his feelings for Leah.

No, there were no answers in the bottom of a bottle of alcohol. There was just the headache from hell. But after that, when the pain in his chest hadn't lessened, when things had only got worse, he'd realized it was too late to protect himself.

And that he didn't want to anymore.

He only hoped that Leah really was here. That Rachel had been telling the truth and Joseph Holt wasn't waiting for him on the other side of the door with violence in mind.

When the door opened, he expected to see a maid. Instead, it was Leah, her mouth dropped open, her eyes round, her skin pale.

She started to close the door, and he put his foot in the way. "No. Leah, please."

"My father isn't here right now," she said.

"That's not why I'm here."

"Then my sister isn't here, either."

"I don't give a damn about where your sister is, and you know it."

She opened the door slowly. "Then what are you doing here?"

"I think the real question should be, why wasn't I here a week ago? Or maybe even, why wasn't I here to say this a year ago? Why wasn't it our wedding from the beginning?" He put his hand on her cheek. "Why didn't I see that it was always you?"

"Because…because…"

"Or maybe I did see. I think I did. I think every time you left me candy, I knew. Every time I listened to you talk about your dreams, I knew. But you were too much for me. For where I was at. So I ran. I made sure it wasn't you. Because I knew you would ask too much of me. I knew you would demand too much. I was right. You have. You have asked everything of me, and you've left me with no more defenses. You are right, you're second to no one, Leah Holt."

"You read my rant in the paper," she said, her voice choked.

"I did. And every word was true. You are not defined by me, by who you are in relation to your sister. You are beautiful. Like no one else. Like nothing else. You're so beautiful it's like staring into the sun. It burns through me. It shines a light in my soul. I wanted to hide from the light, because I knew it would expose me. Because I knew…it would show who I was, and if it did…how could you not turn away? How could anyone not turn away?"

All the years he hadn't felt, all the years he hadn't wanted, crashed in on him now. Threatened to pull him under. He was overwhelmed. By everything. By how much he loved the woman in front of him, by how much he wanted to make it all right.

"Leah, before you I was in chains. I was trapped in a prison I locked myself in so I could be safe. But a prison is still a prison, no matter whether or not you're there by choice. You set me free. You made me realize that all of the stuff on the other side, everything that could hurt was worth it, because the good outweighs it. What good is living life with no pain if I can't feel your arms around me ever again? What good is staying safe if I can never kiss you? What good is anything if I don't have your love?"

"Ajax…you…you said you didn't love me."

"Because I am everything you said. I'm a coward. But not anymore. I'm free of it. Of the fear. There's no room for it. There's just love. It's all that matters. You're all that matters."

"Ajax." She threw her arms around him, buried her face in his neck, tears leaving wetness on his skin.

He wrapped his arms around her, held her tight to him. His wife. The love of his life.

"I thought I knew love," he said. "But I was wrong. I chose to call something love because I found it comfortable. Because it was something I could control, but Leah, that isn't love. I've never known anything like this. So deep. So real."

"I thought I knew it, too. But I didn't really. Not until I *knew* you. Until I appreciated how strong you were. How amazing. Until I knew the hell you walked through, only to come out on the other side."

"Damaged," he said. "I came out damaged. But you...you make me feel new, Leah. You make me feel things in a way that I didn't know was possible. Before it was like I was looking at everything shrouded in darkness but now...now I see it. Now I understand. I thought I knew love, I thought I knew myself. But you found me."

Leah closed her eyes tight, held Ajax. Just held him. And he held her, too.

She was whole now. Her missing piece was back.

"Oh, Ajax. I feel like you helped me find me, too."

"I'm so glad," he said, "because without you, without all of those things you said to me. Without you loving me when I couldn't love myself, I wouldn't be standing here."

"I love you," she said. She pulled her head back, cupped his face with her hands and looked at his eyes. Looked at how they shone with emotion. Not flat, deep. Endless. "Now tell me how you feel."

"I love you," he said, his gaze never leaving hers. "I love you now and always."

"So...all things considered...what if we stay married?" She closed her eyes. "Ugh. I proposed to you again. I have to stop doing that."

He caught her chin with his thumb and forefinger. "No. Don't stop. I like all your propositions."

"Yeah?"

"Yes."

"So...will you?"

"Leah, I'm not perfect."

"I know, darling."

He laughed, then sobered again. "I will fail you. I will make mistakes. I will…I will still growl sometimes. But even then, I'll love you. And if you can take that, that little I have to offer, then I will be the happiest man in the world."

Leah leaned in and kissed him, poured her whole heart into it. When they parted, they were both breathing hard. "Ajax, that's the silliest thing I've ever heard."

"What is? The part about me failing you?"

"No. That sounds honest. You're human, after all. It's the part about you having so little to offer. Ajax, your love isn't a little thing. Your love is *every*thing."

"Oh, Leah, I'm so glad you think so. I feel the same way. Without your love, I would still be chained up inside myself. Without you, I wouldn't even be living. Not really. Your love took all the broken pieces in, and it put them back together. Put me back together."

And then Ajax Kouros, the man of her dreams, looked at her in a way that surpassed her dearest fantasies and kissed her. Kissed her as she'd spent so many days hoping he would. And she could feel it, down to her toes. Because that was the freedom of being exposed. She felt it all.

This was all so much better than any fantasy. Because this wasn't the perfect Ajax of her fantasies who kissed her, then rode off into the sunset with her. This was Ajax, the man, with every scar, every flaw. And more passion than she ever could have imagined.

"So," she said. "I have a silk scarf up in my room."

"I don't need that anymore."

"Who said anything about need? The only thing I need is you. The rest is just fun."

He smiled, the most genuine smile she'd ever seen on his face. "Fun. Something else I was missing, along with love. Leah, I have a feeling with you I'll never be without either one."

"That's a promise."

EPILOGUE

"IT'S OFFICIALLY TIME to panic."

Leah walked out of the bathroom and into the bedroom at her father's Rhodes Estate where Ajax was sitting on the bed, waiting for her.

"Why?" he asked. "Is the bride missing again?"

"Rachel? No. As far as I know she's ready to walk down that aisle with Alex."

It had been a long time since the day Rachel had run out on the wedding that ended up being hers and Ajax's. The best day of her life.

"Then why are we panicking?"

"Well, I know how much you like to plan things. And I know that, after we got ourselves together and thinking straight, we decided to wait a few years to have kids...."

"And?"

"And, well, that's not exactly happening. I just took a test. I'm pregnant."

Ajax smiled, and her whole world brightened, the knot in her stomach dissolving. He stood up and put his arms around her, pulling her against his chest and kissing her, deep and hard, with everything he had. With no control. As he always did.

"That is the best news, Leah. The best gift."

"But...our plans."

"Who cares about plans? The greatest day of my life happened because all of my plans blew up in my face. That was when I found love. It was when I found you. Really found you."

"Thank you so much for not freaking out." She rose on her toes and kissed him again, then relaxed, pressing her forehead against his chin.

"You always surprise me," he said. "I'll never get tired of it."

"That's a relief. Because you're stuck with me for life."

"I always thought that I had to plan every step. That I had to know what was ahead, every facet, every detail, or I would get lost. But I know one thing now for sure."

"And that is?"

"I don't care where my path takes me. I don't need to know what's around every corner. All I need to know is that in the end, I'll be standing with you."

"I promise."

* * * * *

REQUEST YOUR
FREE BOOKS!

HARLEQUIN *Presents*

2 FREE NOVELS PLUS
2 FREE GIFTS!

PASSION **GUARANTEED** **SEDUCTION**

YES! Please send me 2 FREE Harlequin Presents® novels and my 2 FREE gifts (gifts are worth about $10). After receiving them, if I don't wish to receive any more books, I can return the shipping statement marked "cancel." If I don't cancel, I will receive 6 brand-new novels every month and be billed just $4.30 per book in the U.S. or $4.99 per book in Canada. That's a saving of at least 14% off the cover price! It's quite a bargain! Shipping and handling is just 50¢ per book in the U.S. and 75¢ per book in Canada.* I understand that accepting the 2 free books and gifts places me under no obligation to buy anything. I can always return a shipment and cancel at any time. Even if I never buy another book, the two free books and gifts are mine to keep forever.

106/306 HDN FVRK

Name	(PLEASE PRINT)

Address	Apt. #

City	State/Prov.	Zip/Postal Code

Signature (if under 18, a parent or guardian must sign)

Mail to the **Harlequin® Reader Service:**
IN U.S.A.: P.O. Box 1867, Buffalo, NY 14240-1867
IN CANADA: P.O. Box 609, Fort Erie, Ontario L2A 5X3

Are you a current subscriber to Harlequin Presents books
and want to receive the larger-print edition?
Call 1-800-873-8635 or visit www.ReaderService.com.

* Terms and prices subject to change without notice. Prices do not include applicable taxes. Sales tax applicable in N.Y. Canadian residents will be charged applicable taxes. Offer not valid in Quebec. This offer is limited to one order per household. Not valid for current subscribers to Harlequin Presents books. All orders subject to credit approval. Credit or debit balances in a customer's account(s) may be offset by any other outstanding balance owed by or to the customer. Please allow 4 to 6 weeks for delivery. Offer available while quantities last.

Your Privacy—The Harlequin® Reader Service is committed to protecting your privacy. Our Privacy Policy is available online at www.ReaderService.com or upon request from the Harlequin Reader Service.

We make a portion of our mailing list available to reputable third parties that offer products we believe may interest you. If you prefer that we not exchange your name with third parties, or if you wish to clarify or modify your communication preferences, please visit us at www.ReaderService.com/consumerschoice or write to us at Harlequin Reader Service Preference Service, P.O. Box 9062, Buffalo, NY 14269. Include your complete name and address.